I0543183

VENERGY

SARA BLACKWELL

Pants On Fire Press
Winter Garden Toronto London
Madrid São Paulo New Delhi Tokyo

Pants On Fire Press, Winter Garden 34787

Visit us at www.PantsOnFirePress.com

Book design by David M. F. Powers

Cover copyright © 2017 by Pants On Fire Press

The publisher is not responsible for websites (or their content).

First edition 2017

Printed in the United States of America

Library of Congress Cataloging-in-Publication data on file.

ISBN: 978-0982727140

For Dr. Reid

I want to give thanks Dr. Reid who has saved my life in so many ways. Dr. Reid has been spending his valuable time with me every week for years listening to me and providing me wisdom and care. This generous man has changed my life forever. For every displaced American who stated that I am a hero, Dr. Reid is the hero's hero! I adore you Dr. Reid.

I also want to thank God for giving me the words to write and the continuing grace and mercy He daily showers on me.

1

I stood at the back door of the church, frozen in disbelief.

The pews were filled with family and friends, every face a familiar one, and they were all looking to the ceremony taking place at the altar. Kyle was holding Janet's hands. The train of her off-white gown swept around the steps of the altar. Her face was hidden behind a veil, and they only had eyes for each other.

My parents were sitting in the third row. There was room between them and the end of the pew that was saved for me, in case I showed.

Bundles of white lilies lined the pews, and there were petals of roses scattered on the ground by the flower girl. The crowd was dressed in sundresses and jeans with button-up shirts, true small-town formal wear. Everything about the place said that it was a special occasion, a celebration, but sadness hung over it all like a shadow.

There was a missing groomsman and one extra brides-maid. Where the groomsman was supposed to stand was a space purposely left open, a gaping hole in an otherwise per-fect arrangement. The preacher presiding over the ceremony was wearing the same suit he had worn when he presided over my brother's funeral just three weeks earlier.

I slipped in through the door just as Janet finished her vows. It was Kyle's turn. He shifted on his feet, and my heart ached. The preacher asked Kyle to repeat after him before he recited the beginning line. Kyle hesitated on the first word, and then with a shift of his head he looked directly at me.

He had not acknowledged my existence before that mo-ment, and I did not think he had known I was there. However, the moment passed, and Kyle focused back on Janet and briefly closed his eyes. He paused for a second before he recited the vows. The preacher then offered the second line. Kyle, again, looked at me.

This time, Janet followed his gaze and saw me standing in the back of the room in my sports top, running shorts, and tennis shoes. My hair was dragged back into a sweaty ponytail, and no doubt my face was red and shining with sweat. I could hear Janet's disgusted sigh.

Kyle must have heard it too, because he turned to Janet and just stared at her. By now, people were twisting in their seats to see what had caused this unexpected pause. I felt more and more judgmental eyes bear down on me, but in my fear, and in my certainty that all of this was wrong, I did not take my eyes off Kyle.

TWO YEARS EARLIER

We all raised our champagne glasses as Mark Williams, partner of Williams, Wright, & Bishop Law Firm, made a toast to me.

The firm had rented out the entire restaurant at the Ritz Carlton for the occasion. The attorneys—all one hundred of them, the three hundred staff members, and nearly a thousand clients were in attendance, and the press was there to capture the elegant décor and the likewise elegant guests.

A jazz band had set up on the stage in the corner of the massive room, though they now sat with their instruments as they waited for the party to resume. On his way to the stage, Williams had grabbed my arm and unapologetically pulled me out of a conversation I was having with a few clients. He had taken over the band's microphone and called the room to attention before he raised his glass for the toast.

A waitress pressed a glass of champagne into my hands, and I watched as everyone else in the room was handed the same tall flute of bubbly drink.

"Kathleen Bishop," Williams began, "partner, owner, and colleague. You built this firm from a three-attorney practice to what it is today. We are now one of the largest defense firms in Florida. We have the most prestigious clients, and we have been rated with the highest honors by all relevant publications. *You*, Kathy, are the main reason we have been so successful. Not only are you smart—no, brilliant, but you are genuinely honest and caring. You make all of us here feel like we matter to you and to the world. You have dedicated your life to

3

making sure everyone in this room is achieving to the best of his or her ability, and you have encouraged all of us to keep moving forward."

Many of the patrons cheered, and someone yelled, "We love you, Kathy!"

Williams continued. His eyes were fixed on my face, which I knew was flushed with gratitude. "We are so happy that you decided to become the Chief Executive Officer and Chief Legal Counsel to MedVasive. They are truly an impressive company, but they were lesser before you joined them. We know you are going to take them, and the pharmaceutical field, to a whole new level, and we're confident in your great success at your new position. You will be missed." In a wry tone, he added, "And you can come back to work for us if you ever change your mind," to a smattering of laugher.

Williams raised his glass. "To Kathy!"

"To Kathy!" the crowd repeated. Everyone lifted their glasses, then took hearty sips of the champagne.

Mr. Williams hugged me tight and congratulated me. He handed the microphone back to the band, who immediately tapped into a smooth, fast-paced ditty. I stepped off the stage, and one by one, members of the crowd hugged me or shook my hand. The group was full of excitement and kindness, and it swallowed me up. I gulped down my entire glass of champagne and allowed myself to be swept through the throng of congratulators.

It took nearly forty-five minutes for me to make it to the back of the room through the sea of corporate owners, attorneys, and the staff of our firm. I did love all of these people. I truly cared for each and every one of them, and I was sad to be leaving despite the future that awaited me.

I scooped up another glass of champagne and drained it in one motion. I was more than just sad to leave. I was also overwhelmed with worry over my new position. I was good at being a lawyer and getting clients—I did not know if I could be a CEO and CLO. What if the new territory I was entering was territory in which I could not succeed? It was a huge leap of blind faith, and it could ruin my career if I failed.

I grabbed another glass of champagne.

Brenda, my assistant at the firm, sidled up to me and put her arm around my shoulders. She knew I did not typically drink (especially not more than one glass). She leaned in and whispered in my ear, "Worry about the new position and stress over whether or not you'll be successful at it."

I looked at her in disbelief. "What?"

"*Tomorrow*," she finished, and then grinned at me. "Enjoy tonight. This is your night. Kathy. You are the most beautiful person in this room, and everyone here is here for you, so *enjoy* it. Tell your mind that it can worry tomorrow, but you're going to have fun tonight."

I smiled and hugged her. She said exactly what I needed to hear, as always. I swayed a little in the hug as the three glasses of champagne hit me at once. Brenda laughed and walked us to the center of the room, where one of the younger associate lawyers grabbed my hand and pulled me onto the dance floor.

I spent the remainder of the party dancing to jazz music with clients, lawyers, and maybe even a waiter at one point. The rest of the night became a blissful blur.

At around two in the morning, most of the crowd had left, and I was ready to leave myself. The firm's car drove me home, and it was all I could do not to fall asleep in the plush seat. I lived approximately ten minutes from downtown Sarasota in a refurbished wooden home, modest with its red trim and red door, though the lakeside view out the back of the house was anything but.

I thanked the driver, who said he would miss driving me home. Once inside, I shook out my honey-brown hair, stripped off my red dress—the one that swooped down to bare my entire back, and I crawled into bed. I fell asleep thinking of Brenda's advice: tomorrow was the day I would be permitted to worry, but tonight I would only dream of the party.

2

I exited the elevator on the 35th floor and walked to the executive office of MedVasive. I was exactly fifteen minutes early for my first day.

I was wearing my favorite Prada dress suit with long white pearls that I had tied in a knot over my chest. Black four-inch heels with white lining added an extra edge to the outfit, which was my purpose. I could not be confident unless I felt confident in my outfit and my own skin, and I definitely needed confidence here.

The receptionist did not smile at me as I approached. "Good morning, Ms. Bishop. Let me take you to your new office."

With that, she rose from behind her desk and walked me through the hall, which was bordered by large conference rooms, windows that spanned from floor to ceiling, and, strangely enough, intricate paintings that were somehow related to medical procedures, injuries, and MedVasive products.

"Here you are, Ms. Bishop." She stopped and motioned to a corner office. "You have a meeting in Conference Room B at 8:15, but your assistant will be here by 8:00 to go over your schedule for today and to make sure you find where you need to go."

I thanked her and walked to my office, trepidation rising in the back of my throat. The receptionist was gone before I was over the threshold.

The office was easily half the size of my house. This building was on the Siesta Key beach, and the office walls were sheer glass, so I had an amazing view of the beach and the water beyond. For a moment, I simply watched the blue and green shift of the ocean and the speckles of people on the beach. Then I turned away to observe the rest of the space. I had three computer screens on my desk and a shelf that was filled with numbered boxes. In the corner was a small nook with a flat screen television and a couch. Next to it was a coffee table and a refrigerator. In a spark of curiosity, I walked over to the refrigerator and peeked inside.

As I opened the door, I heard a voice say, "We can fill that with anything you want."

I jumped and heaved the door shut as if I had been caught stealing something from my own fridge. I turned to see a blonde young woman leaning in my doorway.

"Sorry to startle you," she said with a giggle. Then she straightened up. "I'm Sandy, your assistant, here to do anything and everything you need, work or personal. I may be employed by MedVasive, but my real job is to take care of you."

I allowed myself to smile. "Thanks, Sandy. I have to admit, I'm pretty nervous. At least I have you on my side."

Sandy's grin lit up her face and her clear blue eyes. "That's the spirit," she said as she waltzed into the office and flopped into the chair in front of my desk. She settled into the seat, scrunching up her blue dress as she straightened out the polka-dotted cardigan that hung over her shoulders.

"First, let's go over your calendar," she said. "Then I'll tell you all about who you're going to meet today. After that, we get to the fun stuff, like what to put in your refrigerator. Also"—she snapped her fingers—"remind me to tell you what you have to do to get Judy, the receptionist, to like you. You'll want her on your side. She can stop people from having access to you. With my help, she'll be in your back pocket by the time we're done with her."

I nodded along as she spoke, but my mind was elsewhere. "Sandy, what are those boxes on my shelf?"

She snorted. "It's all law files and drug files. You'll learn about all of those boxes in your upcoming meetings, and you'll be required to memorize every single detail of every page. Enjoy that."

Sandy then clapped her hands and uttered that it was time for my first meeting. She handed me a leather folder stuffed with a blank legal pad and some papers I had not reviewed. She scooted me out of my office and told me to follow her.

As we walked, she explained that we were meeting the two majority shareholders of the company, who were also

MedVasive's founders and its highest salesmen, Darren and David. "Or the 'Double Ds,' as we call them behind their backs," she said with a smirk. Apparently, the Double Ds were going to explain to me their expectations for me in my new position as CEO/CLO.

Sandy was just finishing her explanation as I was ushered into a massive conference room that sat in the middle of the building, surrounded by windows that looked out into the hall. There was a flat screen hanging from the ceiling and a beautiful arrangement of flowers in the middle of the longest table, of dark cherry wood, I had ever seen. Nestled in the far corner was a kitchenette overflowing with bottles of water, croissants, and what looked like a whole package of different flavors of coffee.

Sandy closed the door behind her, and my anxiety rose along with the two men in navy suits sitting at the corner of the table nearest to the door. Each stood and introduced himself to me, and I smiled and introduced myself in return with forced confidence.

David and Darren were in their seventies or eighties, or at least appeared to be, with their white, thinning hair and wrinkled skin. Both of them physicians and scholars, they had individually written at least one book and multiple medical articles on issues that I could not wrap my head around if I tried.

Under their gazes, I instantly felt too young, the wrong gender, the wrong profession, too stupid and completely inferior in every way, and I hated it. A panicky part of me debated whether I should run out as quick as possible and try to salvage my old job without giving these guys a chance to realize the colossal mistake they made hiring me.

I was jolted back into the meeting when Darren started talking.

"You may know this already, but MedVasive was created for the purpose of finding a cure for brain cancer. When David's wife died of brain cancer, he gave up his practice and dedicated himself solely to finding a cure for that particular type of the disease. He hosted charity events and raised money for his research, and we still have not found the cure to brain cancer, but we have created and manufactured several drugs that have saved lives, relieved people's pain, and given hope to the hopeless."

David, who had been nodding along every few moments, added, "The company's biggest product was a pill that increased blood flow to prevent the need for blood transfusions. That drug made the body create its own blood to replace what it had lost. Another successful product was a series of shots that virtually cured a specific type of blood disorder. The individual can live their entire lives with the blood disorder, but only if the series of shots are maintained throughout their life. It saved the life, but did not kill the disease."

David paused for a moment, and made sure to I look him straight in the eye, assuring him I was paying full attention. He straightened his tie and continued.

"The most recent product MedVasive has launched is a new dissolving vitamin called Venergy. The purpose of the vitamin is to assist the individual in gaining muscle, retaining energy, and, at the same time, burning fat. The prototypes and test cases went from overweight, unmotivated people to toned, energetic athletes. MedVasive has not yet released it to the public, but the publicity plan is already in place.

It was made clear to me that I would be spending most of my first few months on all the requirements of putting Venergy on the market and the criteria we would have to meet to convince the public that they would need the vitamin. I was to analyze confidential testing, research, and information provided by the man who actually invented and tested the product, except that I was not permitted to contact the creator. That was a strict rule.

I was in charge of working with the publicity team, evaluating legal issues that could arise as a result of the product, identifying possible trademark violations, confirming FDA approval, and addressing any potential contractually related matters.

I filled my yellow legal pad with information, transcribing every word I learned from David and Darren. We finished the discussion at lunch time, and the two of them invited me to the country club to celebrate my first day. Despite my expectations, lunch was anything but boring. The older men took turns telling me stories about failed products and their various side effects, both fascinating and disgusting; they even mentioned a medical device that literally caused people's arms to start moving around without their control.

After lunch, we returned to the office. Sandy was waiting for me in that same chair at my desk, and she was eager to ask me how it went with "double D's". As we chatted, I began picking through the boxes on my shelf. I started with the pending lawsuits that I was now taking over. After I was finished, I planned on reading all there was to know about Venergy. I wanted to prove myself with this new product. This was my chance to show the company that I could bring it to the next level.

3

The Saturday morning after my first full week as the new girl, I drove the two and a half hours to the heart of Dade City to see my family. The distance was merely one Philippa Gregory audiobook away.

My grandparents had grown up in Dade City, back when there was virtually nothing to the small town, and their children had done the same, where they met and were married right out of high school. They had known the judges, the sheriff, and the mayor since they all were children. There was nothing that happened in that town that we did not know about, and there was nothing we did that was not known by the entire town.

My parents attended the small Baptist church with the preacher who had graduated high school with me. He was a nice guy, but he had been a wild one in high school. How he mellowed out into the preacher we knew now was a mystery to me. However, anyone can turn their life around—at least, that is what my brother said when we last talked about it.

Joey, my brother, was two years older than I was. He worked at a manufacturing plant as an electrician, a job he had started the first Monday after he graduated high school. He mostly spent the rest of his time playing guitar, participating in a soccer league, or hanging out with his best friend, Kyle Buffington.

Kyle and Joey had been friends since grade school. Kyle's parents divorced when he was in elementary school, and his mother had moved into our neighborhood. She worked a lot, so Kyle had spent every day after school at our house. My mom watched over him, fed him, and made sure he completed his homework. Joey and Kyle were kindred spirits, and together they were so funny they could make the mellow rebel-turned-preacher laugh.

Joey now lived two houses down from my parents, and he came to their house every time I came to visit. We spent every holiday together, every birthday; I spoke to my mom daily and I sent my father my favorite news articles a few times a week. We were always close, and the years had not changed that.

As I pulled into my parents' driveway, I smiled at the sight of my brother's blue Nissan parked outside the house. Philippa Gregory had just finished the last scene of the death of Henry the VIII, my thermos I had filled with tea was empty, and I had a fierce need to use the restroom. I hopped out of my car without locking it or even taking my keys out of the ignition. I rushed into the house, yelling hellos left and right, and I made a beeline straight to the restroom. This was my typical ritual, so I wasn't worried about startling anyone by bursting in.

A moment later, I emerged into the kitchen. My mom was cooking a casserole and my brother was sitting at the table, eyes locked on his phone. "Where's Dad?" I asked as I entered the room.

"He's horseback riding with Larry," Joey responded without looking up.

"Who's Larry?" I asked.

Mom, who was stirring a pot of homemade chocolate on the stove, started telling me about how Dad and Larry had worked together years ago before they ran into each other at Wal-Mart just recently. "You know," she rambled, "what is funny about the two of them…"

Mom kept talking, and Joey looked up from his phone and whispered, "You had to ask." We snickered quietly while she just continued on with her story.

After a few moments, I grew antsy and rose from my seat to go stand next to my mother; I took the spoon from her and began stirring the chocolate. As if she did not even notice the transition, she moved over to the oven, slipped the casserole inside, and filled the rice cooker.

"Mom, why are you cooking that much rice?" I asked innocently. "Are we having company?" I knew the answer, but I felt it necessary to ask to make my point. My mother always cooked way too much food for every meal.

Joey laughed, and she told me to hush.

I set the table for four, asking my brother as I did so for him to play a song for me. Obediently, Joey left the room and returned with his guitar. He reclined back in his chair again and started quietly singing one of his favorite country songs. I hummed along, and my mom continued her work with a look of contentment. I knew how happy it made her to have her children home.

I sat at my usual place at the table after I finished setting out the utensils and everyone's choice drink. Mom was putting all of the food on the table and Joey was in the middle of a silly song he was making up as he went along, when my dad walked into the house.

"Chatty Kathy, laffy taffy!" came his booming voice as he strolled through the door. He held out his arms and stood in one place waiting for me to come to him. I pushed back my chair, and it scratched on the off-white tile floor as I got up and ran over to my father, throwing my arms around his waist. He wrapped his arms around my shoulders and squeezed.

"Okay." I struggled to get out of his grip. "Dad...can't breathe..."

He released me, but I kept a hold of his waist. I breathed in the smell of his clothes, a mixture of sweat and horse. I rested my head on his plaid shirt and told him how much I'd missed him. My mom then told us it was time to eat, and my brother placed his guitar against the wall behind him as we all sat.

"Rodney," was all my mom said, and we all bowed our heads for the prayer that my father led.

As we ate, Joey asked me about the new job and the going-away cocktail party. I talked more than is typical for me about the party, the number of guests and the beautiful dresses.

I also explained the origination of MedVasive and how much I believed in the company and all of the projects I was already running. My brother hung on every word. My parents half listened, but they were less interested in information about my work. They had never really understood it, so they never really participated in any talk about it.

I rushed through my favorite part of my new job: promoting the new vitamin, Venergy, and I expressed my disappointment that my perfect assistant was married and Joey would have no chance with her. When the snickers had subsided, I asked Dad about his excursion with his friend, Larry. Dad chuckled and told us how they had talked about the good old days and galloped around the pastures and checked out one of the neighbor's new corn fields. Then he launched into several stories about adventures he'd had with Larry when they were younger.

After we finished eating, Mom and I cleaned off the table and washed the dishes together. I asked her about her church, her ladies' class, and the upcoming baby showers. She talked as we washed, and I had a thought that this was what peace felt like.

When we were finished with the dishes, I grabbed my mom in a hug and told her I was happy to be home.

Joey followed me outside and helped me carry in my things, including the suitcase I had packed for the trip and a box of files from my office. After unpacking, my brother said his goodbyes and left the house for the night.

I spent hours reading about Venergy, the new vitamin from MedVasive. The things it was claimed this drug could do, ways to make a person strong and energetic, were incredible. The more I learned about it, the more I wanted to promote it to the world.

While I was reading the material from the creator of Venergy, I noticed the creator's name was redacted. I may have been new at the job—perhaps redactions were a commonplace thing—but it seemed odd. As I read further, I noticed that multiple pages were missing. On page nine, the sentence was half finished, presumably continued on page ten, but there was no page ten. The content of the paragraph on page eleven was different from page nine. This occurred at least seven or eight times during my review of the documents. A little irritated, I made sure to add a sticky note to the cover of the packet to ask Sandy to find the missing pages, and then I began reviewing the trial result documentation.

At some point, I heard my parents go to bed, but I kept reading, researching, and taking notes of different avenues for the promotion of Venergy. As I was in the middle of brain-storming, there was a knock on my bedroom window. I nearly jumped out of my skin before I heard a voice whisper, "Kat!"

I shoved aside my research and hurried to the window. I opened it up and saw Joey and Kyle, dressed up and grinning. "Come on, sis," my brother said. "We're taking you out."

"You know, you could come through the front door," I responded, but I shut the window and pulled on jeans and a black silk shirt. I tugged on a pair of heels as I crept out of the house. Out in the driveway, Joey jumped in the back of Kyle's truck, and I took the passenger seat.

"We're celebrating your new job," he announced before he

turned up the radio. We rolled down the windows and we sang as loud as we could all the way to the local bar.

Once inside, Joey and I sat at a table until Kyle returned with beers for the three of us. We talked, laughed, and sang along to the music for hours. I stood up and danced a few times when I just couldn't help it, and the two boys watched and clapped.

At one point, a slow, romantic song began crooning from the speakers, and it wasn't long before a young woman ventured up to us and asked Joey to dance. His face and ears immediately turned a sunburned red as he let her lead him to the dance floor, leaving Kyle and me at the table.

Suddenly feeling awkward, I took a sip of the beer and raised my eyebrows to Kyle as I drank. When Kyle looked down at the table, I glanced around the bar, took another sip, and then did the same.

We both looked up when we heard my brother whistle.

Joey was motioning us to the dance floor. Kyle took a moment before he looked at me and held out his hand; I took it, and we walked to the dance floor. We each placed a hand around the other's waist and held each other's hand out to the side. Our bodies did not touch. I started to giggle.

"What?" Kyle asked.

"Why do we act like we have cooties? I don't have cooties, do you?"

"No," Kyle responded with a laugh. The hands that we were holding we tucked in between our chests. I leaned my head on his shoulder, and he put his chin on the top of my head. I tried to memorize every movement, every touch, as the song played on.

When the song came to an end, Joey went back to our table, and the girl walked back to her group of friends, who all paraded around her, loud and drunk. Kyle and I stopped dancing, but we stayed in the same position for a few seconds after the dance was over. Then the moment was gone and we pulled away from each other. We finished our beers, and left for home.

It was one in the morning by the time Joey and Kyle dropped me off. They said they would see me at church in the morning. I thanked them for the great time and jumped out of the truck. I snuck back into my parents' house and went straight to bed, giddy and unable to stop smiling.

4

I woke the next morning to the smell of coffee and bacon. I rolled myself out of bed, slipped on my shoes, and grabbed my keys and wallet. Joey was eating bacon at the table when he saw me. He jumped up and said he was coming with me. He wiped his greasy hands on his dress pants and followed me out the door.

"Really, Joey, you have a napkin," I commented as he laughed at me. Mom walked over to the table for Joey's plate and did not bother to ask where we were going. She knew. We were headed to Starbucks for my daily iced tea.

Joey and I returned with my tea and his plain coffee with sugar (despite my objections to the added sugar). He was constantly trying to lose weight, to watch his diet and to exercise, but he just could not stay consistent, and always kept a belly. I thought it was adorable. Mom and Dad were already ready for church and waiting for us to get home so we could leave. They were at the kitchen table, sitting and patient, but my mother's pursed lips told me to hurry.

I rushed to the bathroom, straightened my brown, shoulder length hair, applied eye liner and lipstick, and hurried into my bedroom to throw on a black fitted dress and heels. I presented as plain, but classy. It took me hardly ten minutes to rejoin my family in the kitchen.

Our small town had three churches: Baptist, Catholic, and Presbyterian. No others. There may have been small groups of other religions that met in people's homes, but the majority of the folks of the town went to one of the three churches. The lone exception was if there was a wedding or a funeral. Then the whole town went to the church where the event took place, regardless of affiliation.

We arrived just before the service was to begin. The pastor was at the door, greeting everyone who entered with a handshake. A few other families were shuffling into the building along with us.

"Well, I'll be," said Pastor Steve with a smile as we approached. "If it isn't Miss CEO, Kathy Bishop." He hugged my neck, then squeezed my shoulders as he let me go. "Still no Mr. CEO, I take it?" he commented with a wink.

"Stop it," I said with a smile, and we walked through the doors into the foyer. I hugged and was hugged by adults and kids I had known my whole life. There was something satisfying about being surrounded by people whose love you have known since you were a child.

Piano music started filtering out from the auditorium, an indication for the moms to bring their kids to the nursery and the adults to find their way to their seats. I was moving along with the crowd while looking around for my family, whom I lost during all of the hugging. I saw Joey close by, so I pushed my way toward him. That was when I spotted Kyle by his side.

It was no surprise to see the two of them together, no matter where they went. Even after high school, when Joey had gone to work at the plant and Kyle had gone away for pharmaceutical school, they had constantly been in touch. As soon as Kyle finished school, he returned to Dade City and took over the local pharmacy. It was in the only grocery store in the city, and so everyone in the town came to Kyle for their medicine and for medical advice. With his sweet and loving spirit, he was a perfect fit for the job.

"Kat!" Kyle said, his blue eyes bright. Today, his short blond hair was clean and cut, so you could tell where it was starting to bald in the back. He grabbed my arm and pulled me to him, and I stayed in his arms as long as I could. No one called me Kat but Kyle, and it had been my nickname since childhood.

To be honest, I adored Kyle, maybe too much. As long as we had known each other, we always remained friends, and there was never anything else. However, there was one night, maybe a year ago, when Joey was away and Kyle sat with me on our porch swing. We just talked. We talked about ambition, being scared, making mistakes, our true desires for families of our own. He sat a little too close to me. His hand rested half on his leg and half on mine. After hours of talking, I rested my head on his shoulder, and we just swung in silence for nearly another hour. Then, as if he'd had a sudden realization, Kyle jumped up and said he needed to go.

We never had any other intimate moments until last night's dance, which may not have been considered anything close to intimate to him. But I had not forgotten our moment on the swing, and I often wondered what it meant to him.

Kyle, Joey, and I found our usual third-to-last row pew and sat next to my parents. The choir began singing, their voices swelling in the room, and I forced myself not to think about Kyle or work or anything.

We returned to my parents' house after the service, and before my mother could force me to eat lunch, I packed my car and left for home. I wanted some time to go over another box of Venergy documents before I went to work on Monday, and I wanted to do some much needed house cleaning.

By nine in the evening, I had floors that shined, toilets that were spotless, laundry cleaned, and clear windows. I also reviewed the box I had set my sights on before. It was full of results from several different research facilities. All of the preliminary reviews of the results were very promising. The drug itself had very few side effects. Some of the animals tested were reported having shaky movement or chills if given too much in quantity. Few had diarrhea, but it only lasted the first few weeks of taking Venergy.

In the human trials, the side effects were similar: diarrhea, shakes, chills, and occasional vomiting. There were a small percentage of human participants who experienced rashes, and others who passed out a couple of times if they took Venergy without eating. Otherwise, from my initial review of the records, the drug was very safe.

I grew more and more energetic about promoting the drug the further I read. I could not wait to see it out in the public. I wanted to get FDA approval as soon as possible and get samples for people I loved. It was becoming possible that my first pharmaceutical product was going to be a great success.

5

Six months after starting at MedVasive, I oversaw the settling of three cases in litigation, I negotiated five contracts, reviewed multiple documents, and I submitted a request to the FDA for approval of the new vitamin. As CEO and CLO, I was also in charge of the agenda and the presentations of meetings. I spent nights preparing for conferences, and I was attending them several times a week.

For the first few weeks, standing in front of employees, shareholders, partners, competitors, potential clients, and company directors was incredibly nerve-wracking. After that, I soon realized I was good at it. I made sure I was the most prepared person in the room. I made sure I was the most knowledgeable about whatever topic was being discussed. I had to learn specific details about medical illnesses, drug side effects, doctors' needs, and economical and accounting issues specific to each product. I quickly learned that the manner of the presentation depended entirely on the audience.

Sandy, my assistant, had a hard time keeping up with my pace in the beginning, but she quickly fell into the rhythm of the way I worked. We started early and ended late. We skipped lunch, she took at least two Starbuck's runs each day for us, and we took a midmorning spin class across the street. She swiftly became indispensable to me.

Approximately two months ago, I was concluding a presentation to Darren, David, and the Board of Directors. They thanked me and started to gather their handouts and writing pads to leave, but before they could get out of their seats, I requested the chance to speak about one more thing not on the agenda. Everyone sat still and did not agree or disagree to stay. They simply waited for me to speak.

I smoothed my black pencil skirt and tried to stand as tall as I could in my snakeskin heels. "I know I have only been here a few months, but I want a raise." I paused to allow everyone time to panic. I smiled and added, "Not for me. For Sandy."

Their stares were blank, disbelieving, but I plowed ahead. "Sandy was an assistant to the general counsel of the company before I started. She worked forty hours a week answering phones, typing dictated letters and pleadings, and retrieving documents whenever they were requested. She is now the *executive* assistant to the CEO/CLO. She appeases our number one clients when I am unavailable. She learns fast, and I could not do what I do without her. Her hours are nearly as long as mine, and yet she has nothing close to the benefits of my position."

The group was listening, and they looked convinced enough, so I went for it.

"I want her salary doubled, with quarterly bonuses depending on our productivity."

The director sitting next to me huffed. An officer dropped his head and shook it while staring at the table. I saw someone's nose scrunch and another push back his chair from the table.

"Look, you hired me to do a job. I need her in order to do it. We are not paying her a fair salary for the responsibilities she currently undertakes."

The grouchiest in the room asked, in an incredulous grunt, "Bonuses?" Perhaps he agreed with doubling the salary, but was not sold on the bonuses. This at least gave me a negotiation point.

"What about double the salary with bonuses discussed at the end of each year? And it is still dependent on our productivity?"

I crossed my arms and went silent, focused on remaining staunch and unmoving. There were a few quiet private debates among the members. Some just sat and stared at me, maybe waiting for me to withdraw my request or storm out of the room. I did not budge.

After a few minutes, one of the board members said, "All in favor of this proposal, say 'aye.'"

Silence.

Silence.

"Aye."

It didn't take long for another voice to follow, then

another. My excitement rose, and within two minutes, I had the agreement of the entire room. I smiled and thanked the group, all the while doing a mental victory dance and pumping my fists in the air.

After that meeting, I met with Sandy in my office. I thanked her for her service. I acknowledged her long hours, her quick learning skills, her discretion and dedication. I explained to her that I was going to expect more and more from her. She was good, but I wanted her to continue to grow just as I wanted to continue to grow. Then, when she was both flattered and wary thanks to my sudden proclamation, I told her about her salary change and bonus structure.

Sandy did not keep her victory dance internal. She leaped out of her chair and danced around my office, shrieking in delight. Her blonde hair bobbed up and down as she pranced in circles.

I allowed her a few minutes to have her fun, then I told her my list of tasks I needed completed by the end of the day. The list took up six pages, and it was already 4:30. In the face of such a list, I thought that Sandy may change her mind about the raise, but she smiled and said she would finish the list before she left for the day. Her spirits were not dampened in the least.

6

"Yes, Dr. Oz, I've been taking Venergy myself for about a month. I lost two inches of fat, gained lean muscle, my appetite is suppressed, but I still feel the need to eat regularly. The best part is that my energy has increased dramatically, and my ability to sleep soundly is more than enjoyable."

Sandy slipped into my office and placed my iced tea in front of me. She also slid two small files onto my desk with a blue note stuck on top. Blue notes were messages from men. It was our system. White notes were messages that were purely work related. Yellow notes were related to family or friends, and red meant it was an emergency.

I smiled up at her as I listened to Dr. Oz's questions regarding research and FDA approval of Venergy.

"Yes," I replied, "we just recently received FDA approval.

It's going to be available to the general public in one month. We have already been sending samples to dieticians, physicians, and gastroenterologists. We received all positive feedback. The only reported side effect from the samplers was too much energy in one patient who had an eating disorder."

I had been pushing for a spot on the Dr. Oz show for weeks. It would be great advertising and an exceptional way to introduce the product. But, more importantly, it was my first step to convincing Oprah Winfrey to try the product. The shareholders and board members said it could not be done. I responded that there was nothing I could not do. There would be obstacles, it would be difficult, maybe impossible, but I could do anything I decided I was going to do. I received the same reaction from everyone. Laughter.

But I did not laugh with them, and I wholly intended to prove myself by obtaining Oprah's endorsement.

Dr. Oz agreed to have me on the show to discuss Venergy. He thanked me for the samples that I sent to him every day for four weeks, and agreed that the "guinea pig" at his office who was using it was very happy with the results. We agreed that Sandy and his office would confirm the particular dates and plan for the show, and we hung up the call.

"Sandy," I called out before taking a sip of my iced tea. She skipped into my office moments later, her blonde ponytail swaying. Without being offered it, she threw herself into the chair in front of my desk.

"We got the Dr. Oz show," I said with a cocky smile.

Her eyebrows shot up. "Really?"

"One step closer to Oprah," I continued, leaning back in

my chair with my newest pair of black and silver heels crossed and propped on my desk. The smile on my lips quickly puckered as I started to think.

Sandy must have noticed my change in attitude, because she snorted and said, "It's been a whole ten seconds and you are already planning your next move? Enjoy this victory. You'll get Oprah. You know it, and I know it."

I sat up and asked her if she really thought so. She just gave me a huge, toothy smile. That was when I noticed the blue note on my desk. It was a phone message from Perrone, a brown-haired, Southern physician who had asked me to dinner after I met with him to discuss Venergy. I accepted his offer, and it had been a lovely dinner. He was polite and treated me with complete respect. Unlike most doctors I knew, he spent more time asking about me than talking about himself.

The note said that Perrone had called "AGAIN" and asked for a meeting next week, any time after work. I threw the note in the trash and sat back in my chair.

"So what's wrong with this one?" Sandy asked.

I smirked at the question and shrugged. "Nothing that I can find," I responded, my eyes flickering to the other files on my desk.

Sandy just kept watching me, clearly waiting for me to divulge more. After a few moments, I looked up and met her stare, challenging her to force it out of me.

It didn't take her long.

"I had a great time with him," I finally said, though I could hear the lack of confidence in my tone. "He's handsome, he's smart, successful, polite…"

She looked unconvinced. "And? When do you explain why you're avoiding him?"

I hesitated. "And, and, nothing. I would love to go out with him again, I guess. I just feel like dating is a chore. I analyze every detail for days after we go out, every time. Then I worry whether he likes me, if I like him. I don't get butterflies when I see Perrone. I don't get excited when I see his name on my phone or one of your notes. I always hoped for those fairytale feelings of being in love, but I don't have them."

Sandy watched me thoughtfully for a moment, before commenting that sometimes those feelings took time. "It's not always love at first sight, you know. The more you get to know each other, the more you might feel the butterflies."

"Maybe," I murmured. "But I guess I don't find it worth the effort. I am busy and I'm happy…enough."

Sandy laughed and offered that I had enough options. She was constantly running out of blue note cards, so she was sure I would find the right guy at just the right time. I couldn't help but smile. There had seemed to be a stream of available and interested men since I started my position at MedVasive, but none of them had held my interest. I blamed it on being too focused on work.

Sandy left our conversation at that and returned to her work. After a few minutes of silent contemplation, I started working on the new files she had brought to my office.

7

After a long day, I drove home to an empty house. I pulled myself out of the car and dragged my handbag inside. I ambled straight to my room, stepped out of my shoes, and stripped off all my clothes. I collapsed onto my bed and stayed there for several minutes without moving. I let my chest feel crushed as my heartbeat filled my ears.

I was happy for my recent successes, but felt like I was just lucky. I felt like a fraud, as if they would soon figure out I was not confident or smart or skilled. I feared an inevitable Big Screw-up that would end with a news story and my job lost.

After nearly thirty minutes of lying motionless, I decided I had to pull myself together. I pushed myself off the bed and changed into a sports top, shorts, and running shoes. I strapped on my white visor and grabbed my phone and earbuds on my way back out to my car, my mind set on the beach.

As soon as I arrived at the shoreline, I stuffed in my earbuds, turned up the music, and ran.

It was evening, so most people out on the sand were dressed in regular clothes, waiting for the sunset. I ran past the tripods with cameras facing the west. I dodged kids playing in the sand and watched lovers cuddle on a blanket near the water. I ran until it was completely dark, except for the moon and its reflection on the ocean. Then I turned around and ran back. Halfway to my car, my body started to feel weak, like sludge, and my face began to tingle.

I stopped running and walked the remainder of the way back down the beach, trying to regulate my breathing along the way. With each slow breath, I prayed, I thought about priorities, and I put myself back in a place of peace. As long as I was doing what I felt God wanted me to do in a truthful, honorable way, then I was successful. Even if I screwed up or I was fired, I was a success if I stayed the course for which I was meant.

That was a speech I gave myself multiple times before I was completely calm. Once relaxed, I realized just how hungry I was. I made it to my car, drove to the nearest Mexican restaurant and ordered enough food to feed a family of four. After eating as much chips, beans, and cheese as my stomach could hold, I went home for a shower, eager to crawl into bed and collapse from exhaustion.

As I was driving home, my brother called. "Joey," I answered. "What's up? How are you?"

He said that he was fine and work was great and nothing new was going on. Oh, except that Kyle was engaged.

My heart stumbled in my chest, and it took me a moment to respond. "What?"

"Yeah. He met this girl, Janet, a few months ago. He said she's really nice and she wants to get married, have kids, all that. He said he doesn't think he knows her well enough to make that big of a commitment, or if he's even ready to start a family, but Janet's really pushing for it. I guess he's cool with it."

I pulled into my driveway, but I stayed in the car, letting it idle. "What?" I replied as I stared out at the garage door. "I mean, that's crazy. Don't you think it's crazy? He can't marry her." I stopped talking, and Joey started to say something, but I interrupted him. "He's being stupid. He is such a typical stupid man."

"Wow," my brother responded. "Kathy, I know you guys have always had a thing, but you never dated. Maybe cut him some slack?"

"We never had a 'thing,'" I bit back.

"Whatever." My brother ignored my denial. "Kyle has always asked me about you. He always comes to Mom and Dad's house when you're over there. You always ask about him when we talk. I have suggested to *both* of you that you go out on a date, and you both have excuses for why it would never work."

"It wouldn't work," I responded defensively.

"Then why do you care if he gets married? Be happy he found someone who wants a family with him."

I was angry and hurt and I had absolutely no right to be either. "Fine, Joey, I'll be happy for him. I would love to meet this Janet person…girl…family-starter."

"Great. I'm throwing them an engagement party this Saturday, and you have to come." He paused. "Please."

Against my better judgment, I agreed to come home for the weekend. I thanked my brother for the call and we hung up. I rested my forehead on the steering wheel and sat in the car for another few minutes. This whole day had felt like a rollercoaster ride, and not the good kind, but the kind that makes you sick and takes forever to end.

Regardless, it was late and I had a court hearing at 8:30 the next morning, so I needed all the sleep I could get. I forced myself out of my car, got ready for bed, and tucked myself in. Surrounded by pillows in my pitch-black room, I was sound asleep in seconds.

8

It was Thursday, and I was only listening with half an ear to our visiting scientist, who was giving an incredibly lengthy presentation on a new drug he was trying to sell to MedVasive. My head was nodding toward the table; all I wanted was to lay it down for a few minutes. I felt a nudge on my left arm and I turned to Darren. He gave me a pointed look. I recognized that look. My mom gave me it whenever I got the giggles in church as a kid—it meant *pay attention.*

I faked a smile at Darren and started flipping through the packet the speaker had handed out to go with his presentation. The packet was more like a book. It was a two-inch thick pile of grafts and photographs and plenty of extremely large words.

This man had created a drug he named "Molly." It was still in the research phases and would not be complete for a few more months. *Then why am I here?* I thought. *Come back when your research is complete.*

If the drug worked as he expected, it would completely and wholly cure Acute Lymphocytic Leukemia (commonly called "ALL"). ALL was the most common cancer in children and teens. Based on recent statistics, 85% of children with early diagnosis of ALL could survive past the seminal five year mark. If the child lived past five years from the diagnosis, then they would likely live cancer-free for the remainder of their life. The current treatments for children diagnosed with ALL included a variety of very painful and devastating drugs and therapies, not limited to chemotherapy and radiation. The children undergoing treatment were weak and miserable for several years. It was a disease that affected not only the child, but the entire family.

"Molly is a vaccination given to a child between the ages of six months and a year," the speaker rattled on. "The vaccination would prevent the child from contracting ALL and would significantly lower other forms of cancer in the subjects who take it. It would save the child's life and keep the child from experiencing years of pain and suffering. It would also save the family both heartache and money.

"The parents would be given the option of providing the vaccination to their children, but our hopes are that it becomes a governmental mandate for all children."

There was one significant problem that the scientist said would be the biggest obstacle to FDA approval and drug distribution. One element of the vaccine was Ecstasy. The element was not Ecstasy as a whole, but molecules of Ecstasy were included in the vaccine. It would be a hard sell to the government and to the public to inject people, especially children, with something imbued with Ecstasy. He said he could not imagine a mother purposely injecting Ecstasy in her six-month-old baby with no family history of leukemia.

So now we're in the business of creating crack babies, I thought. There was no way this was something we could attach to our business name. It was way too controversial and socially unacceptable.

"Um, excuse me." I raised my hand. "I appreciate your work and it sounds incredible. The Board needs to meet about this, but I am fairly certain MedVasive will not be taking part in this vaccine."

I started to stand to leave the meeting. I heard enough, and I had too much work to do to let this scientist waste any more of my day. Darren, however, grabbed my arm and yanked me back into my seat before I could take my leave. I didn't have to look at his stormy expression to know he was unhappy with my interruption.

"Ms. Bishop, please, give me five more minutes," the man begged. "Just five minutes." He turned off his presentation, for which seemed to be only halfway through with. My face burning, I apologized for the interruption and asked him to continue his speech.

"Ms. Bishop, there are a lot of strange and scary things in a lot of drugs currently on the market. Many drugs are poison. This vaccine is no different, except that it contains a known and socially unacceptable illegal drug. Thus far in our research, rashes, redness, and small fevers that subside after a few days are the only side effects of the vaccine. It has prevented leukemia in every subject, animal and human, that has taken it. This drug can save thousands of lives in the United States alone every year, and the cost of continuous manufacturing would be relatively low. With all due respect, Ms. Bishop, this is a miracle, and it would be criminal for us to ignore the results because of one element of the vaccine."

Ignoring whatever expression Darren was wearing, I stood up again and nodded at the speaker. "Thank you. We will discuss it, and I promise to read the information you handed out. We will contact you as soon as a decision is made." With that, I grabbed my pamphlet and walked out of the room. I made sure to shake the man's hand on my way out.

I walked past Sandy and straight into my office. "Did we schedule the Dr. Oz show?" I called back to her. "Send me the date or the reason we don't yet *have* a date. Did we submit the final responsive information to the FDA on Venergy? Tell me yes or provide me with the reason that it has not yet been done and who is at fault for it. Please, schedule a telephone conference with opposing counsel on the Johnson case so I can tell them our final settlement offer."

"Oh, yeah," I hollered as an afterthought. "Call Perrone and ask him if he'll come with me on Saturday to a redneck engagement party in Dade City."

I then spent hours going through emails, mail and returning calls from my voicemail. I was bothered by this Molly drug. I couldn't shake it. I was preparing a response to a request from the FDA on one of our older drugs, and my mind would drift to images of doctors inserting Ecstasy into sweet, crying babies. I had to shake my head to scatter the thoughts and get myself back on task. I also cursed myself for not being more on the ball and asking the scientist how he actually knew whether Molly prevented the disease, or whether it had ever been tested on children.

"Two weeks from Friday is your appearance on Dr. Oz for Venergy," Sandy's voice said from the doorway. She was leaning against the frame with a yellow pad in hand. "The responsive packet on Venergy went to the FDA yesterday. You have a telephone conference on the Johnson case in fifteen minutes, and you have a meeting with the MedVasive salesmen in thirty minutes that you requested last week. Remember, you wanted that meeting to discuss tactics for selling several of our products. I put your folder for that meeting on your desk while you were out. And Perrone said he would be honored."

She flashed me a grin. "Anything else?"

"No, Sandy. That's perfect. Thank you." I gave her a weak smile in return, and I opened up my file for the Johnson case to prepare for the conference.

Fifteen minutes later on the dot, my phone rang.

"Hi, this is Kathy Bishop," I answered to opposing counsel. Without waiting for a reply, I offered, "We are two months from trial. Your client has no real medical injuries or damages. She cannot prove her damages. We are giving you our final settlement offer right now. You have one week to accept it, and we promise that we will not settle before trial if not accepted in the stated timeframe. We offer $10,000 to settle with a full release. I will follow up this conversation in a formal letter, but I wanted to tell you verbally in case you had any questions."

Johnson's attorney replied that he understood and needed

to speak to his client. We ended the call moments later.

I could care less whether he accepted the offer or not. If he accepted the $10,000, it was one less task and problem for me. If he did not, then we would go to trial. Trials made me nervous, but they were great experiences. They were a message to the public that MedVasive did not just hand out money to anyone who claimed injuries from our products. We were fair and offered fair money when we were at fault. But we were not going to put up with false claims of injury, and trials were a powerful way to make that known.

I grabbed my file and rushed to the conference room where the twenty MedVasive salesmen were waiting. These salesmen each supervised fifteen or more MedVasive salesmen, so in this meeting alone I was going to be talking with many different strains of our marketing system. I sat at the head of the table and began discussing techniques of selling the company products. I wanted a conversation with all of them so we could all learn from each other, teach each other, and come up with new ideas in a way that would satisfy as many of them as possible.

At the end of the day, I left with my Molly pamphlet. Once home, I made myself a massive bowl of cereal and read the entire thing, long into the night.

I found I could not stop reading it. The research and the results of the trials were nothing less than incredible. The presence of Ecstasy in the vaccine was explained in such a way that made it appear even safer than most antibiotics and chemicals people put in their bodies on a daily basis.

By the end of the book, I was a true believer in Molly. I

even considered whether we could make it a required vaccination for all babies, like rubella and polio. That would be an issue for later down the road, but the information I had been provided was amazing. Our speaker hadn't exaggerated; this drug was a miracle. The crucial issue would be to use the terms of the elements of Ecstasy and not the word Ecstasy itself, take the focus away from the insinuations and place it on the truth of the vaccine, and what it could accomplish.

I fell asleep with the pamphlet crushed under my arm as the sun rose outside, an hour until I had to be at the office.

9

Friday morning, as soon as I walked into my office, I requested Sandy schedule a meeting with Darren and David in the conference room. I asked her to tell them to bring their Molly pamphlets with them.

I walked into the meeting to see the "double D's" laughing to themselves, no doubt ready for some Molly bashing. David joked that MedVasive was not into making crack babies. Then he started mimicking a baby on crack. Or, he tried. Really, he just looked like an old man having a seizure.

"We are doing Molly," I announced, totally serious.

"Yes, sure," Darren drawled.

"Guys, I'm serious. Did you read the pamphlet? This drug is far beyond what we originally thought it was." I kept talking despite their dumbfounded faces. I told them about the statistics of children who suffered and died from leukemia. I explained how the Ecstasy ingredient was less dangerous than many of the ingredients in chemicals such as chemotherapy and other drugs that were used and accepted by the public. I told them about the animal testing results and the preliminary tests that had been conducted on infants. "This drug is not only going to virtually wipe out adolescent leukemia, it's also going to make this company trillions of dollars."

Darren was worried about the press. He said that it could destroy the company. He'd had a bad experience with some negative press in the past, so he was hypersensitive to any potential damage the media could cause.

"There could be bad press," I acknowledged.

Darren voted negative to Molly. He did not want to take the risk, even though the possibility of the money was tempting. He warned me that he would advocate to the other Board members to vote against the drug.

The process of new products began with Darren, David, and me. If we all agreed on it, then it went to the Board members. If it passed by a $3/4^{th}$ vote, the majority shareholders would vote. If it passed the shareholder vote by 51%, then the company would purchase ownership of the product. In the contract that I would prepare, we required the original creator of the drug to sign a waiver giving away any and all rights to the product. He or she could not even discuss it without MedVasive's permission. Most importantly, the creator had to dedicate two years of their time to training our employees on the manufacturing of the product, the science behind it, and all research which was conducted for it. It was a lengthy and very expensive process from beginning to end.

Without Darren's support, Molly would not even go to the Board.

"Can you at least give me more time to investigate?" I offered. "I want to meet with the scientist behind it and talk to him directly. If this drug turns out to be as great as it sounds, then I will make a deal with you."

Darren huffed at that. "What kind of deal?"

"If I decide this drug is worth backing, then we all support it. If it turns out to give us so much bad press that MedVasive's stock value decreases significantly, I will personally go to the press and tell them that this was my idea and that the Board and shareholders were not aware of the dangers or elements of the drug. You can put out a public statement terminating me for my actions."

Darren and David looked at each other, then back at me. Darren shook his head and breathed out heavily through his nose.

"I will consider it. You do your investigation, and if you can convince me, then we will schedule the Board meeting to vote on Molly." Darren stood up to leave, but not before adding that he thought I was crazy.

David winked at me and followed Darren out of the conference room.

I stayed in my seat for a few minutes. Was I really willing to give up my career and reputation for this product? Why was I so sure that it would save so many people just because of one book?

Risks are inevitable, I thought to myself, and that was that.

Finally, slowly, I stood, gathered my things, and walked back to my office. I stopped by Sandy's desk on the way.

"Can you schedule a lunch for me with the scientist from yesterday?"

"You mean the creator of Molly? His name is Dr. Reed."

"Yes, him. As soon as possible, if you could."

"I thought everyone was against that product." She glanced at me for a moment, and then she shrugged dramatically. "But I just work here, so what do I know. Now that I'm looking at it, your calendar is so full that you are not available for lunch for the next four weeks." She met my eyes again with a grimace.

I waved my hand dismissively. "Move things around. Make it happen next week."

"Of course." Sandy casually chewed her gum and she pulled her hair over her left shoulder. "Now, what do you really want? Why are you just standing there?"

I tilted my head back and stared at the ceiling. "It's Friday," I groaned.

"So?"

"I have the engagement party for Kyle tomorrow. Remember, I'm taking Perrone with me?" I sighed and gave Sandy a flat stare. "I don't want to meet this Janet person at all. Plus, my family is going to be doting all over her and talking about how great she is. I'm going to have people talking to me about how I'm still single and everyone else is getting 'married off.' The whole thing is going to be torture in every way."

Sandy's face was pitying, even as she smiled. "Yeah, but you'll make it through. If you can go head-to-head with the Double Ds every week, this party's going to be a piece of cake."

49

I snorted, and then strolled on toward my office with a halfhearted wave in her direction. When I made it to my desk, I threw myself into my seat, and before I could start fretting about the party some more, I saw a red note on my desk. Red was code for "absolute emergency."

I was immediately thrust into triage mode for the remainder of the day. A doctor who was one of our largest buyers had put out a press release that one of MedVasive's older products caused his patient to suffer irreparable harm to his leg, which had been amputated at the hip to prevent further damage. Negative press was not unheard of, but this particular article was in a large enough publication that it needed to be addressed, and quick.

10

Perrone picked me up on Saturday at noon. He stepped out of his Porsche and walked to my door just as I was coming out. He took my bags from me, kissed my cheek, and asked if I was ready to go.

"I am, but are you sure you want to do this?" I asked as I locked my door and followed him to the car.

He only responded with a laugh. He opened the passenger door, I climbed in and he placed my bags in the small pocket of space behind the two seats. Then he settled into the driver's seat and hummed, "Off we go," as he backed out of my driveway.

Off we go, I thought with a grimace. I was nervous to see Kyle and to meet Janet. I was worried about Perrone meeting my simple family, a man who came from a physician mother and brain surgeon father. I had no idea why I decided it would be a good idea for Perrone to come with me. He was so excited, and he thought it was quite significant that I wanted him to meet my family. I felt a little bad that I was giving him false impressions of the state of our relationship, but it was too late now to change my mind.

The first few minutes of the drive were quiet. The top was down on the Porsche, so the wind blew over us and tossed my hair around as I watched the buildings and trees whiz by. I decided to settle my mind and to stop worrying about anything. I wanted to have a good time, and I knew Perrone did not come with me to watch me sulk.

I turned to him and asked him how his week was. He smiled and told me about a few surgeries that he had conducted and a new client that he anticipated would be a legal problem. That conversation segued into Venergy and how passionate I was about the drug. I really wanted to tell him about Molly, the number of babies that could be saved, and the controversy of the Ecstasy ingredient, but that was completely confidential information. Molly could not be discussed until it was formally a MedVasive product.

Perrone offered that he used the Venergy samples I gave to him and he could definitely tell the difference. He said he would promote it to patients and other doctors. I thanked him. I told him that I was bringing home a bag full of samples for my brother, Joey. In response, he asked me about my family and my home life.

I spent much of the drive telling Perrone about my childhood, the small-town life, and inevitable, Kyle snuck into the conversation. When I spoke about him, Perrone's interest seemed to peak. He looked at me as I described Kyle and was completely silent as I explained the closeness that my family felt toward him. He laughed at my reaction to his questions about Janet. It was evident that I utterly despised the girl even though I knew nothing of her. Perrone suggested I was jealous of Janet, and I just snorted.

"I am not jealous. I'm just concerned for someone who's like a brother to me being pressured into a marriage with a woman he barely knows. What kind of person asks a man to marry her after knowing each other only a few weeks? Sounds kind of desperate to me."

Perrone shrugged. "Who knows, you could love Janet. She could become like a sister to you. Don't judge it, or her, until you see it for yourself. It seems like you care about Kyle quite a lot—you're just worried because you care. You're a sweet person, Kathy, and honestly, I can't wait to meet your family."

He placed his hand on the console between us, and after a moment, I placed my own hand over his. Perrone was kind, and he seemed to care genuinely about me. Maybe Sandy was right. Maybe all I needed was time to get to know him. I turned and looked at him, curious if I could ever actually love him. He must have felt my stare, and he turned and looked at me. He smiled and turned his hand over so our fingers laced together.

"I'm glad you're coming today," I said to him, and I meant it.

We drove the last thirty minutes of the drive in silence, holding hands. It was peaceful with the wind and the radio playing low in the background. I started to look forward to being with my family and giving my brother the Venergy samples. Perrone and my dad could hang out and bond over cars, and I could spend time with my mom. Maybe my brother could play some music for us. I ignored the whole engagement party in the last few moments before we made it home.

"There it is." I pointed to my parents' house as we drove down the dirt road. "And that's my brother's car."

Perrone laughed at my excitement. "Don't you come here almost every weekend?"

"Yes, but I still love it. Besides, it's the first time I'm bringing a guest," I added for his benefit.

We pulled into the driveway, and I leaned over Perrone and honked the horn. I wanted my dad to come outside and see the car. I knew he would love it. After four beeps, my family piled out of the house. I climbed out and stood against the Porsche, leaning my butt against the passenger door with my arms crossed like I owned the thing.

Sure enough, my dad whistled and walked over to us with his eyes bulging. He squeezed me in a brief embrace before immediately roping Perrone into talking about details of the car—the origin, the year, the model, all things I didn't care about in the least. My brother just rolled his eyes and hugged me.

"I have a gift for you," I told him. I reached behind my seat and grabbed the bags of Venergy. "Here. Take it every morning and afternoon and let me know what you think."

My brother thanked me, and then slung his arm around my shoulders, walking us over to Perrone. "Joey," he said with a smile, and he put out his hand. Perrone shook my brother's hand and introduced himself. That was the total of their conversation. My brother turned me around and guided me into the house. I could hear my mom telling Perrone she could help carry in the bags since I was so rude just to leave him out there. I turned to see Perrone and my mom carrying bags behind us while my father ogled over the car for just a little longer.

The moment we walked inside, my happy family time ended. The house was covered with trays of finger foods and decorations; the furniture was all moved to the sides, and a huge cake sat on the kitchen counter.

"Mom, what is this?" I asked.

"The engagement party. Did you not know we were having it here?"

"No," I said with a huff. "Why is it here and not at Janet's parents' house?"

No one answered. Joey busied himself with pouring a packet of Venergy into a water bottle. My mom ignored me. I rolled my eyes, and then I told Perrone he could sit at the table and I would get him something to drink. I rushed to the restroom, as was tradition, before I returned to bring our bags to my room.

"Honey," my mom yelled across the house. "You don't plan on sleeping with this man under my roof, do you?"

"*Mom*, please," I screamed back at her. "No. Of course not."

After dropping off the bags, I trudged back into the kitchen and mouthed *sorry* to Perrone. He smiled, but it was definitely strained.

"Joey," I called, trying to save the moment, "did you know

55

Perrone is the youngest physician in all of Florida, ever?"

My brother sidled over, acting politely interested, and asked him how he got to his position. Perrone began to go through his educational background, and Joey pretended to listen, and things seemed to be going fine. Then the door opened. I turned, expecting my father, but instead Kyle stood in the doorway.

My heart sank with sudden nervousness. It was frustrating that my comfortable feelings toward him could change so dramatically just because some stupid girl wanted to marry him. Two weeks ago, when he walked into the house, I jumped out of my seat and hugged his neck. Now, I was paralyzed and mortified. Perrone was still talking to my brother, but he looked at my face and could see there was something wrong. He stopped talking mid-sentence and turned in his chair to see who had walked into the room.

Kyle locked eyes with Perrone, confused, and the two of them just stared at each other. My mom stepped away from her last minute preparations to see Kyle. "Sweet baby Kyle," she cooed as she ran over to him and wrapped her arms around his neck. This broke the stare-a-thon between the two guys. Perrone looked back at me, and I smiled as best I could.

Kyle hugged my mom back and thanked her again for throwing the party. He reminded her that she did not have to do it, but she told him that he was family and she would do it for any of her children. Then she conveniently added, "Neither of those two kids will ever get married, so at least I get to host one engagement party before I die."

"Hah, hah," I responded, deadpan, as I forced myself to

stand up and walk over to Kyle. I went to hug him, but we both leaned into the same side and messed up the hug, adding to the awkwardness. I ended up just patting his back and moving away from him. Usually, he would have cracked up and tussled with me had we fumbled with a hug any other time, but now he just stood there. I couldn't stand it.

Perrone rose from his seat and politely introduced himself. They shook hands, and Kyle quickly asked Joey if he could go with him to the store. "I need a new tie for tonight," he announced clumsily.

Joey, seemingly unperturbed, finished his Venergy water, grabbed his sunglasses, and rushed out the door with Kyle without a word to anyone.

Perrone and I decided to drive around Dade City so I could show him my old high school and where we all used to hang out when we were kids—anything to get out of the house. We promised to be back in time for the party, and I all but dragged him out to the car.

11

After the tour of all 3.2 square miles of the small city, Perrone and I parked near a lake and settled in to talk. We just sat and watched the rippling water, enjoying each other's company. After an hour of peace and quiet, we left and headed home for the party, but not until after we took a Starbucks detour. Perrone had the same addiction as I.

When we arrived back at my parents' house, there were cars everywhere. Neither of us was dressed for the party, so we decided to sneak in the house through the side door to hide from the guests. Perrone ran to the bathroom with his clothes, and I changed in my old room. Fifteen minutes later, the two of us emerged from our respective rooms and walked in to the party hand-in-hand, like a real couple.

Perrone looked sharp and a little out of place in his light

green Armani dress shirt, matching tie, and khakis. I was wearing a fitted mustard yellow knit dress that stopped mid-thigh. It went perfect with my dark brown wedges and my long pewter pearls.

We walked down the hall and into the cleared living room space that was filled with people I had known my whole life. I hugged and kissed everyone around. No one waited for an introduction—everyone just grabbed Perrone, hugged him, kissed his cheek, and talked to him as if he was an old friend. Women were telling Perrone stories about me when I was a child and what a rascal I was during my middle school years. He and I were eventually separated by the sea of people pulling us in opposite directions.

I was laughing with my good friend from high school, Holly, when I noticed Perrone and Kyle talking across the room. I completely stopped listening to Holly, and my mind strayed, thinking about what on earth they could be saying. I felt myself melt into a nervous wreck. Perrone was smiling and seemed to be making casual conversation. I could not see Kyle's face, but he was rocking his body back and forth.

Holly must have asked me a question, because it wasn't long before I realized she was just staring at me expectantly. I tried and failed to find the correct reply. "Excuse me, Holly," I blabbered. "Sorry, but my date is asking for me over there."

I pushed my way through the crowd and utterly ignored calls of my name and guests trying to speak to me. But in all my determination, I did not see the man in my path until we collided in the middle of the overcrowded living room.

He grabbed my arms to steady me and prevent me from

falling backwards. I looked up with an apology on my lips when I realized it was Kyle. I was rendered speechless. I just stared into his blue eyes as he held me up by my arms. Neither of us said a word for several moments. He looked as if he was going to say something, but in the end, he just stayed silent. He helped me upright, and then we simply stood there, unsure of what to do or say. That was when I noticed a pair of arms being wrapped around Kyle and a set of hands grasping the front of his shirt.

Kyle yanked his hands off my arms and placed them on the palms that were resting on his stomach. A red-haired beauty popped up from behind him, smiling as if she had won the lottery. I instinctively took a step back and offered her a sad excuse for a smile. She walked around Kyle, keeping one arm around him and holding out her other hand. "I'm Janet," she said.

I shook her hand and told her I was Kathy, Joey's sister. She made a comment about my parents' house being "cute" in a tone that made me feel insulted. Then, completely oblivious to the implications of her comment, she snuggled her nose against Kyle's cheek and asked him if he was ready to cut the cake.

"It is a *sweet* cake," she said. "But, a homemade cake at an engagement party is a bit tacky, don't you think?" Her fiancé cringed as she spoke. I let out a long breath, muttered that it was nice to meet her, and escaped to find Perrone.

Janet might have had beautiful red hair and adorable freckles, but it did nothing for her personality. Of course, I knew nothing about her, but, frankly, I didn't want to.

Joey met up with me as I searched for my date, and he commented that he'd noticed my meeting with Janet. He must have noticed my irritation, because he gave me a look and asked, "Did you even give her a chance?"

I raised my eyebrows and jabbed my finger at my brother. "Yes, and in the two seconds I was around her, she insulted our parents' house and the cake Mom spent two days making for *her* engagement party."

Joey laughed and told me to lighten up; I punched him in the stomach and told him to be more protective of his family. Perrone walked up to join us then, and I was actually glad to see him.

"How are you handling all this?" Joey asked him as he winced and rubbed his middle.

"It's nice. Everyone's very nice, and they all want Kathy to marry me and have babies. Like, all of them," he said with a laugh.

Joey chuckled and hugged me tight. He told Perrone that was the way this town was and how it had always been. "They give my sister a hard time because she's a working woman instead of a baby-maker. All the other girls her age from Dade City already have two or three children, and she hasn't even hit puberty yet."

I stomped on my brother's shoe and told him to shut up.

A call from my dad came from the kitchen for all the guests to gather around. In a few moments, the crowd that had taken up every room was crammed into the kitchen. Joey swiftly pushed his way to the cake and the engaged couple. My mother stood to the side, beaming at the sight of her beautiful creation. I felt sad for her, knowing that the guest of honor did not appreciate her work. For a second, I imagined shoving Janet's face in the cake and making her appreciate it.

As Perrone took my hand, my brother began to speak to the crowd. "Kyle is my best friend," he began, "and he's also a brother to me. I'm more than happy that he found someone he wants to spend the rest of his life with. Every single day. Forever." Joey paused as the crowd chuckled. Kyle looked directly at me, and I raised my eyebrows and pursed my lips. Janet stood next to him, beaming bright.

Joey finished the speech with a congratulations, and my mother swooped in to cut the cake as the crowd applauded. I rushed over to assist my mom dish out slices of cake onto plates, and Perrone handed them around to the guests. Kyle stood next to my brother, shoving cake in his mouth and loudly praising it so that my mom could hear. Janet sat down at the table and mushed the cake around, but I never saw her take a bite.

After cake, everyone continued to mingle and slowly leave the party. Janet was one of the first to go—she announced that she hated to leave a party that was thrown for her, but she had to wake up early for a wedding dress shopping excursion. The crowd showered her in excitement and forgave her for leaving early. She kissed Kyle and left the party with a few other girls.

I started helping my mom clean as the party thinned out to a mere few guests. Perrone was lounging on the couch next to my father, neither of them speaking to each other or anyone else. I walked over to them and gave them permission to go to bed. I praised them both for a job well done and kissed them both goodnight on the cheek. Perrone thanked my mother, shook hands with Kyle and my brother, then slipped away to my brother's room where he was sleeping. My dad disappeared without a word to anyone.

Joey and Kyle sat at the kitchen table talking, and everyone else left. I chatted with my mom as we washed dishes, picked up paper plates and cups, and wiped everything clean. Neither one of us mentioned Janet at all, likely because Kyle was right there at the table. I complimented my mother on a beautiful and successful party as we finished cleaning, and she hugged me tight. She said her goodnights to Joey and Kyle before she too disappeared.

I grabbed a water bottle and sank into the chair between the boys. "Do either of you want anything?" I asked.

Joey answered that he did want something, but it was at his house and he was leaving. With that, he rose from the table, kissed my forehead, waved goodbye to his friend, and left. There I sat with Kyle, in the aftermath of his engagement party.

Kyle quietly commented that Perrone was smart, considerate, and a great catch. I smiled and said that Perrone was a great guy, but we were friends, and he was just gracious enough to be my date for the party.

At a loss of what else to say, I told him Janet had pretty hair. Kyle snorted out a laugh. I had no doubt that he knew exactly what I meant. His laughter broke the tension, and the conversation changed to the state of his pharmacy. We also talked about my new job, and Venergy. I did not mention the Molly drug because I wanted to talk to him about it at another time, when I could really ask his advice, and when I could explain the confidentiality aspect of the issue.

We talked for over an hour before an awkward pause finally snuck in. Silence. Kyle looked at me and I looked at him. I searched his eyes for something, anything.

I said, "Congratulations on getting married, and all. I know you must really love her if you plan to marry her."

Kyle huffed out air and muttered, "Yeah," but he left it at that. He stared at the table. I sat there in the quiet.

He's marrying Janet, I thought. *He won't even ask me out on a date. I'm pathetic. If he liked me, he would make it known. I'm tired, and I am wasting my time with a guy who is already engaged. Maybe our "moments" are nothing to him. Maybe he never felt anything for me at all.*

Abruptly, I stood up and told Kyle I was tired. I thanked him for the wonderful party and congratulated him again. I did not hug him or go near him. I only smiled as I said goodnight. I turned and walked stiffly to my room before he could reply. If I were polite, I would have walked him out or at least waited to leave the kitchen until after he left, but I did not want to hope for a "moment" or special goodbye and just be disappointed instead. So, I just walked away.

My head was a mess when I climbed into bed, but thankfully it didn't take me long to fall asleep. As soon as I woke, I packed and put my things in Perrone's car. I stomped through the house loudly to wake up Perrone, which worked marvelously. When he stumbled out of my brother's old room, I told him I needed to return to Sarasota for work.

He packed his bag, made his bed, and was ready to go in minutes. We hugged my mom and dad and ignored my mom's fussing about skipping church and my dad's desperate invites for Perrone's (or his car's) return. We drove back to Sarasota, where I spent the entire day working on the Molly and Venergy products.

Perrone went home after he dropped me at my house. He kissed me goodbye, but I pulled back before the kiss turned too deep. I thanked him for putting up with my family and me, and for being my date. He said he hoped it wouldn't be the last time, and he looked forward to seeing me soon. I agreed, however halfheartedly, and he drove away.

Perrone was being more polite than sincere, I could tell. The weekend had proved to both of us that we were not on the road to a relationship.

12

"Venergy is a new revolution," Dr. Oz announced to his audience. "This is the real thing. This vitamin, added to your water every day, does not make you lose weight. It gives you the energy you need to work out. It gives you the hunger for healthy foods. It helps you rest at night so you can be at your best each day. Venergy turns the average American who has no energy, who eats terrible, and who does not get proper rest into a healthy and energetic person."

He allowed a moment for applause, and then he continued.

"Please welcome the CEO of MedVasive, the company that created of Venergy, Kathy Bishop." He held out his hand to the left side door of the stage, and I walked out as I was directed by the stage-hand in the back.

The crowd cheered, and I smiled at them as I came across

the stage, squinting against the bright lights. There was a sign lit up at the side of the audience that said APPLAUSE. That made me feel less flattered by the great welcome, but it also made my smile change from a fake, nervous one to a real, genuinely amused grin.

I sat in a chair next to Dr. Oz and smoothed out my cream Versace dress suit. He guided me into a discussion of the benefits of Venergy, the extremely low medical risks, the affordable price of the product, and the real-life examples of the changes Venergy had already made in people's lives. There was a tall, round table in between us, atop which sat a bottle of water, a packet of Venergy, and a glass.

As we spoke, Dr. Oz poured the vitamin and the bottle into the glass. He drank it while I took the lead on the conversation.

"I gave this product to my brother nearly three months ago," I said, pride evident in my voice. "He has taken it every day since. We talk regularly, and he tells me that he is eating healthy and he is always into some new fitness addiction. You have to know my brother—he has always lived life without any concern for health, fitness, or proper eating. Now, he can't get enough exercise, healthy food and good sleep. His entire physique has changed in three months."

"Well, it says a lot to me, as a doctor, that you would recommend this product to your own family. That shows you really believe in it," Dr. Oz commented, and the audience murmured in agreement.

I sat forward in my seat and readied myself for the chance I was about to take. "I believe in it so much that I have a challenge. I have a challenge I want to reveal on your show."

"All right, let us hear it. You have us all in anticipation of this *challenge*." I noticed the camera move close to my face to capture a close-up of my response.

"I challenge Oprah Winfrey to try this product for three months. I will supply her with the product for free and will have it delivered to her if she accepts. If she tries the product for the three months and gives it her stamp of approval, then we will put out free samples to everyone in the United States who signs up through the MedVasive website. If Oprah does not like the product, we pull it from the shelves and we will never sell it again."

At this bold comment, the crowd went wild. They could not believe I placed so much on one person's opinion.

"That's a lot of responsibility for Oprah Winfrey, don't you think, Ms. Bishop?" Dr. Oz asked, skeptical.

I agreed, but I told him I believed in this product, and I believed in Oprah's ability to distinguish a quality product from one that is not worth selling. "If she does not experience positive results from Venergy, then I don't want my company producing and selling it."

Dr. Oz commented that he would be interested in knowing whether Oprah would accept the challenge. After the commotion over my announcement subsided, I answered questions from the audience, and we discussed the ingredients of the vitamin. Dr. Oz announced that every member of the audience would receive a week's supply of Venergy, and then we went to commercial.

I thanked him for having me on the show, and he told me

I was crazy. I laughed and told him that my whole company kept saying the same thing. He said he would love to have me back, especially if Oprah accepted the challenge. It would no doubt be good for ratings. I told him I agreed, and I thought he should do what he could to convince her to accept the challenge. He shook his head with a knowing smile. He seemed to understand perfectly.

After the show, I returned to work. Sandy jumped out of her seat as soon as she saw me.

"Oh, my God, Kathy! Social media is blowing up about your challenge to Oprah. You've caused so much press and talk about Venergy. You were *brilliant*. The hits on our site have gone through the roof since the interview. Awesome. Just awesome."

She could not stop talking about it. I smiled and continued on my way to my office to start on emails, FDA documents, and one legal case that was very active at the moment. Sandy followed me into the office and was blabbering on and on about the entire thing. I mostly ignored her while reading emails, but I did catch comments about how thrilled Darren and David were, and that I was being praised around the office as the queen of MedVasive.

I told Sandy I was as excited as the next person, but I had to focus on getting the Board and shareholders to agree to purchase Molly, and also deal with the emails and cases in front of me. "I can't stop just because I had one good interview. I have to keep going."

Since the meeting in which Darren had refused to approve of the drug, I did more research, visited the facility, watched the drug being created, and met extensively with the scientist behind it. I finally convinced Darren and David that Molly would save the lives of thousands of children, and the controversy would be small compared to the benefits. They were both on my side now, and with the newfound information I had, I believed I could convince enough of the Board members and shareholders to pass the required percentage of voters. The first meeting with the Board was in two days, and I wanted to be completely prepared.

Checking my emails, I saw that I had one from Perrone. I had not seen him in over three months, since the engagement party. We had spoken and sent messages a few times, but it was as friends and colleagues. It was nice—there was no need for a discussion about what we were to each other, or about our future. We just fell into a stress-free friendship.

Perrone's email said only, "You are crazy, but you got her. No way she could decline with the fuss you created. I'm impressed!"

I responded that I was "crazy, that was for sure, and I never doubted that I could get her to endorse the product. You can't stop me from getting what I want. Haven't you learned that yet?" I ended the message with a smiley face.

Immediately after, I called opposing counsel on the Johnson case, which was now scheduled for trial in less than two months. I wanted to go over some details of exhibits, motions, and other issues related to the trial.

While I was on the phone, Sandy threw open my door. She was smiling and making all sorts of impatient noises under her breath. "Sorry, can you hold on a minute? My assistant is having a seizure in my office," I said to the man on the other line, and then I muted the phone. "What in the world are you doing?"

"Oprah put out an official statement that she accepted your challenge. She ordered enough Venergy for three months to be delivered to her home, and she promised to begin first thing tomorrow morning. Dr. Oz wants for you to return to the show in three months, and Oprah will be there to tell you her decision." Sandy squealed as she ran over and hugged my neck, almost squeezing the life out of me.

I was lost for words—I couldn't believe that Oprah had accepted so quickly, or that she had accepted at all. It was all going exactly as I had planned. I laughed with Sandy and at her pure excitement. She deserved this as much as I did. She worked so hard with me on Venergy, Molly, and all of my other responsibilities. Sandy was fully invested in my work, and this was a victory for her as much as it was for me.

After giving myself a few moments to catch my breath, I unmuted my phone and finished my call with the Johnson opposing counsel. We spent over an hour discussing evidence issues, which documents were admissible, motions to be filed, and monotonous litigation tactics. The entire time, I wanted nothing more than to quit the call and give myself some more time celebrate. As the man on the other line was discussing the final issues of which experts were going to testify, I noticed I had a red notecard on my desk. Scrawled on it was a message that said my mother had called. She wanted me to get back to her immediately.

I stopped opposing counsel in the middle of his sentence

and told him I had an emergency and that I would have to call him back. I hung up on him without waiting for a response, and I hit my mother's speed dial. She picked up after half a ring.

Before she could say a word, I asked, "Mom, what's wrong? Are you okay?"

My mother's voice was full of fear, and it made me feel cold. "It's your brother. He collapsed at work. He has a very low blood count. He's in the hospital, but we aren't allowed to see him yet. The doctors came and told us the real problem is determining what caused him to pass out. They said it could be as simple as dehydration, or he could've had heatstroke, or he could have a stomach bug. But it could be something very serious, so they're running a bunch of tests on him right now."

I started crying before she was finished. My gut told me it was serious. Something in my heart told me things were not going to be all right. I told my mom I was on my way and that I would see her in a few hours. She did not have to tell me in which hospital he was. There was only one in Dade City.

I had no clothes, no toiletries, nothing. I didn't know if I should run home and pack a bag or just go straight to the hospital. I did not have any work prepared to take with me. Without knowing what to do, I grabbed my keys and my purse and I left. I did not see Sandy on the way out. I did not say anything to anyone. I got in my car and I drove.

The two-and-a-half-hour drive felt like six days. I kept my phone on my dashboard, waiting for a call from my mom. I did not turn on the radio. I had my windows rolled up and I drove in complete silence. My thoughts were all over the place in worry and anticipation of what I would find out when I arrived.

I prayed. I prayed constantly. I begged God to make it a cold or a stomach bug, something small. I knew that God's will would be done regardless, that His plan was the perfect plan even if I did not understand it, but I told Him that *I* wanted my brother to be okay. I thanked God for His faithfulness. I told God I would love Him no matter the results of the tests. I promised that I would worship and trust Him regardless of the diagnosis, but I begged and begged for my brother's health.

Just as I was pulling into the parking lot of the small hospital, my phone rang. It was my mom. She said they were just wheeling Joey into the room now, Room 200. I parked and ran into the hospital, up the stairs, and to Room 200.

My parents were sitting on the bed beside where Joey was lying. Tubes were poking out of his arm where he was receiving IV fluids. He looked very pale. The doctors were in the room talking to my family when I barged in. Everyone stopped and looked at me.

I threw myself on my brother's chest and just hugged him. My mother stood and walked toward the window in the little hospital room. She was facing away from my brother, her shoulders shaking and her breath heavy as she cried. Dad was holding my brother's hand, and the tips of Joey's fingers were white because my dad's grip was too tight.

Unable to deal with it all, I sat up and eyed the doctors. "So, um, why did he collapse today? Do you have a diagnosis yet?"

There were two male doctors in the room. The older said

that he had already explained to my parents and to my brother that Joey had esophageal cancer. They could not know how extensive the cancer was until the upcoming surgery, but from the information they had managed to obtain, it appeared to be incredibly aggressive.

I wanted to throw up.

I could not breathe.

My world, my perfect world, came crashing down all around me with every word out of their mouths. I started having pain in my chest. I did not move while the doctors finished speaking to all of us about the upcoming surgery, chemotherapy, radiation, and plans for proceeding with his care. I was in a trance, half-listening, half-denying that any of it was real.

As soon as the doctors left, I curled into my brother's bed with my head buried under his arm. I cried so hard that one of the nurses poked her head in to check on us. My mom kept asking me to stop crying. My dad patted my shoulder and told me that I was upsetting everyone. Joey held me as tight as he could and he encouraged me to cry all I wanted. How could this happen to him? Why *him*? I wanted to scream.

I cried until my body was out of energy, until the nurses came in and asked me to move so they could take Joey's vital signs and check his IV. I pushed myself out of his bed and trudged over to my dad, who was sitting in a chair in the corner. I sat on his lap and I rested my head on his shoulder. No one said anything as the nurses prodded Joey. My brother was staring at the ceiling. He mostly just stared at the ceiling the entire time.

A minute after the nurses left, there was a knock at the

door. "Come in," my mom called in a voice scratchy from crying. It was Kyle who walked into the room.

My mom had likely kept him updated just as she had with me. He was still wearing his uniform, so I could only guess he was coming straight from work. Kyle looked at Joey, who was still staring at the ceiling. Joey turned his gaze to his friend. Neither said a word.

Kyle walked over to the bed and wrapped his arms around his best friend. This was the first time Joey had cried in the time since I had arrived. Both of them cried as they held each other tight. Kyle told Joey he would be fine and that we would all take good care of him and help him beat this stupid disease. He encouraged Joey and tried to give him hope, but it wasn't just my brother he was lifting up. It was as if Kyle brought a glimmer of hope and light into the entire room.

After Kyle let go of Joey, he hugged my mom, and my dad stood to embrace him. Then Kyle came over to me. We had not spoken since I walked away from him at the kitchen table after his engagement party. I had purposely avoided him at my parents' house and at church since that time. But all of those silly emotions were irrelevant now. Kyle took me in his arms and held me close to him. I buried my face in the crook of his neck and I cried. I felt comfortable with Kyle in the same way I felt comfortable with my brother. I could be vulnerable, ugly, a mess, without worrying about anything.

As much as I loved them, my parents made me feel that I should hold in my feelings, put on a fake smile, and pretend everything was fine when it was not fine at all.

"Think of this cancer as one of your projects," Kyle

murmured in my ear. "You have to beat it. You have to win."

My parents were sitting on Joey's bed while I was hugging Kyle. We were alone in the corner of the room, with my parents talking to my brother about how he was feeling and what they were going to do to get him home as soon as possible.

Kyle pulled out of our embrace and held my face in his hands. I looked at him, and I felt strange. I wanted him to stay with me, to help me through this. I wanted him to love me and take care of me, and to help me take care of my brother. I wanted him to kiss me and tell me everything was going to be all right.

Kyle kissed my forehead and told me we would all make it through this and that he would be by our sides the entire time. I smiled as best I could and thanked him. The two of us then joined my parents at the foot of Joey's bed. We talked for several minutes before the doctors returned.

They announced that my brother was scheduled for surgery to remove the cancer on Monday morning. He was being released to go to my parents' home until then. They would have more information for us and options for moving forward after the surgery was complete. The operation would reveal to them the severity and pervasiveness of the cancer. They apologized for the bad news and gave their permission for my brother's release from the hospital.

We took Joey to my parents' house and got him settled. It was nearly midnight by the time we had my brother in bed and asleep. Kyle was leaving, and I decided to go back to Sarasota too. My parents and Kyle tried to talk me out of it, but I could not be persuaded. I was still in my suit, and I had work to do.

I planned to finish the week at work and return to Dade City after my Board meeting regarding Molly. I would stay for the surgery and until Joey was released again from the hospital. What I did not tell them was that if I did not keep busy, I feared I would fall apart.

Kyle walked me to my car and asked me to drive carefully. He asked that I text him when I got home—he said there was no way he could sleep until he knew I was safe. I promised him, then I turned to get in my car. Kyle grabbed my arm and pulled me into him. He hugged me. No, he held me.

He did not say a word, just held me for a few seconds. I squeezed him tight and I breathed in the smell of him. I was emotionally exhausted, and this embrace felt more calming than anything had all day. It was too soon when he let me go and said goodbye.

I drove home in silence. Again, I prayed, but I felt defeated.

13

The next day at work was brutal. My head felt as if it was going to explode, and my eyes burned. My spirit was numb. I walked into my office in a daze, and Sandy ran over to me.

"What happened to you? You disappeared. You could have been dead." She touched my cheek with her hand. "Actually, you look dead, honey. Are you sick?"

I kept walking despite her barrage of questions. I sat in my office chair and opened my email. There were nearly a hundred emails with red exclamation points indicating that they were immediate issues. I had a stack of phone messages, and my voicemail light was blinking. I dropped my head on my desk and sighed long and loud. My nose was squished on top of the phone messages.

Sandy stood at the door and informed me that she had

been working hard to find the missing pages in the information from the inventor of Venergy but could not locate anything, and no one knew anything about it. She added that the Double Ds did not recall the name of the inventor of the product—it seemed so unusual that such vital information would not be maintained. She promised to keep trying to get to the bottom of it. On her way out, she commented that she was going to Starbucks for my tea and that she would bring me back a variation of medications.

I stayed silent, and she left.

Kathy, you can make it through a few days, I thought. *Take it one day at a time. Do not even think about Dade City. Focus on work. Focus on your job. Do not fall apart. God will push you through until the end of the week. You can do this. Can't stop, won't stop! Yes, that is my mantra. Can't stop, won't stop.*

I sat up and forced myself to start with the emails. I returned phone calls as I scoured through my email. When Sandy returned with my iced tea and a plate of pills, she looked puzzled by my whirlwind of activity. I winked at her as an expression of gratitude for the tea and pills, but I was on the phone and typing all at once, so I could not give her anything else. Sandy merely shrugged and left my office.

As I was finalizing a settlement of the Sanson case that involved a broken IV needle, I opened an email from Jennifer Smith. The email said that she was Oprah Winfrey's personal assistant. She had received the Venergy. Oprah was excited to try it out, and she planned on tweeting about her progress for the next three months. She told me that I would likely not hear from Oprah at all until the day of the Dr. Oz show, but if I had any questions, I could contact her in lieu of talking to Oprah herself.

Dr. Oz and Oprah's endorsements would assist me in getting a wider range of celebrity support. I had a list of people I wanted to join them in endorsing this vitamin. I was contacted by four people on my list, asking me for samples. I told them they could have full access to the vitamin as long as they went public about it on social media. If Oprah endorsed Venergy, I was going to go ahead and contact the remainder of the people on my list.

I finished the day preparing for the Board meeting and attending a regular meeting with Darren and David to discuss updates on various products and legal issues. They were excited about the settlement of the Sanson case, and they were beyond satisfied with the attention Venergy was getting. They agreed to promote Molly at the Board meeting on Friday as a reward for all that was taking place at MedVasive since my arrival. They indicated that stock was up and that the shareholders had nothing but great things to say about MedVasive and the new CEO.

I called my family every single evening after I left work. Joey sounded tired, but hopeful. My mother did not want to talk about the cancer at all. We had stilted conversations about cooking and flowers and did not mention my work or my brother. My dad spoke only of news stories, but he also started texting me articles on esophageal cancer. They were all miracle stories. I presumed he had also found articles discussing the high death rate, and the torturous treatment for the cancer that only prolonged the life of the patient for a few years, just as I had, but there was not one negative word from my father about the cancer or my brother's prognosis.

I was able to remain busy all week and accomplish all my requirements at work through Friday. That afternoon, I stood in front of the Board members with my on-screen presentation and handouts on the drug Molly. I had made sure beforehand to structure the presentation in such a way that the controversy over the Ecstasy element would hardly be noticeable. I was confident, and I wanted this product now even more than before. I knew this drug would not save my brother, but it could save kids from experiencing at least one type of cancer, and at that moment, that was all I could ask for.

The presentation went so well that it surpassed my expectations: every single Board member voted in favor of the drug, and they all agreed to devote their time and support for the shareholder meeting that was to follow the next week. If the shareholders voted for Molly, we would purchase the product and it would become my project. The biggest hurdle would then be getting FDA approval even with the element of Ecstasy in the vaccine.

After the unanimous vote, my entire audience, including the Double Ds, stood and clapped for Molly. They were calling out accolades about saving children, about the miracle drug that would be God's gift to suffering families. I thanked everyone, grabbed my things, and left the meeting as soon as I could.

I returned to my office and collected two boxes filled with documents and a laptop that I had asked Sandy to gather for me during the meeting. She and I carried the boxes to my car, and I left directly from work for Dade City. I had packed the night before, so I had all I needed to stay with my parents until Wednesday. Earlier in the week, I explained everything to Sandy, and we had coordinated a way for me to work remotely from Dade City. There was a great possibility no one would even know I was away from the office.

I grabbed a smoothie on the way out and started toward Dade City. I was not in the mood for an audiobook, and I did not feel like having my typical hip hop thudding in my ears. I blared the gospel station loud the entire drive. I wanted to fill my spirit with His Spirit. I needed to feel close to my God or my head and heart would be blown to pieces.

I was very happy about Venergy and Molly. I was proud of those two products, and I was enthusiastic as to where and what those drugs could do for the company and for the citizens we served. Venergy could help people get fit in a healthy way, and Molly could save the lives of so many young children who would suffer and die otherwise. I headed to my home with prayers of thanksgiving and hope, but also with a heavy heart and fear for my brother.

14

I hugged Joey and kissed his face as the nurses in blue scrubs wheeled him out of his room.

"I love you. You will be great. It's going to be fine. We will be praying." I was talking fast, holding his hand and running alongside the gurney. My father grabbed my shoulder and pulled me back. My hand slipped out of my brother's, and I stopped in my tracks while Joey disappeared behind a pair of windowless double doors at the far end of the white hall.

That was forty-five minutes ago. Since then, I had been sitting in the waiting room in silence. My father read the news on his tablet. My mom made small talk with one of the other ladies in the room. Kyle sat next to me. He whispered to me that everything would be fine. I did not respond. I did not even acknowledge his comments. He eventually stopped talking.

At one point, I got up and asked the nurse the location of the bathroom. I stepped into the single stall and stared at my face in the mirror. My heart felt like someone was squeezing it so tight it would bust. My stomach churned, and my breath was going shallow with worry. This surgery would tell us whether my brother would live or die, and if he was going to die, how long until he did so. All of a sudden, I felt very hot. I felt weird. I took off my shirt and saw that my stomach was soaked with sweat. My face began to tingle, and black spots filled my vision.

I didn't remember falling.

I didn't know how long I was out, but I woke up to the sound of banging on the bathroom door and Kyle's voice calling my name. My mind tried to come to life, but I could it felt like ages before I could peel my eyes open. After that, I convinced my mouth to respond to Kyle. "Just a minute," I mouthed, but no sound came out. Then I threw up. I had no control over my body, so I just vomited all over the tile.

I guess Kyle could hear me throwing up, because within seconds there were nurses opening the door and hovering over me on the floor. I was mortified that Kyle was there watching me, shirtless, lying in my own vomit. The nurses were murmuring things, and I was helped onto a gurney. They placed a sheet over me to cover my upper body. Once in a room, a nurse put an IV in my arm and started me on fluids and a strong dose of Valium.

By that time, I could speak, but my body was so tired and so heavy that I could not move. It was embarrassing, and I felt awful that I was making such a scene when we were here for my brother. My eyes started swimming with tears that I was unable to wipe away—and I had thought this couldn't get any worse.

A doctor came into the room and began to ask me questions about stress and anxiety. Then he asked me what I had eaten in the past week. He told me I was very dehydrated and that my body had grown weak beneath unchecked stress. He recommended I stay on the IV for at least twelve hours, and that I begin a regular regimen of Valium and an anti-depressant for a brief time.

Kyle came into the room then. My parents did not follow, and I assumed they were waiting for Joey's results. The doctor excused himself as soon as Kyle entered, and I turned my head away in shame. The tears dropped over my nose and down my cheek. There was a wet spot on my pillow under my face.

"Kat," Kyle said in a soft voice. He sat on the bed next to me. "Look at me, please."

I turned my face to him, and he looked me in the eyes. He wiped away a tear from my cheek. He said that Joey was out of surgery, said that it had gone well, and that he should be released from the hospital in two or three days. Kyle was smiling as he petted my hair softly, but it looked forced. I knew there was more.

"What?" I asked. "Just say it."

He swallowed. "They cut this big mass of the cancer out of his stomach, and they had to take a major part of his esophagus. They're still testing the lymph nodes to determine how far it's spread, but the doctor said it was extensive. In the next couple weeks, Joey will have to start doing chemo. It won't cure him, but it will help him live longer."

"So it's terminal?" I asked.

"Yes." Kyle looked to the floor and put his hands in his lap. I could see a tear fall onto his pant leg.

"How long?" I whispered, my throat clogging up.

He Kyle did not answer immediately. He sat with his head slumped, unmoving. Then he said, "The doctor estimated less than a year."

I turned away from him again. I rolled up into a ball just as I burst into tears, and I cried as hard as my body would permit. It was ugly, painful. I screamed and cried while Kyle sat next to me. He placed his hand on my back, but he did not move otherwise. I could hear him sniffing in between my deep, shaky breaths. When I could control myself enough to speak, I turned around and asked Kyle, "Will you hold me?"

Kyle climbed into the bed with me, and I rested my head on his chest as he wrapped me in his arms. He stroked my hair and rubbed my back until the tears stopped. We stayed that way for hours. Nurses came in and out to check on me, change my IV bags, check my vitals and insert more medication into me. My mom and dad came in to tell us that Joey was still sleeping and would likely not be awake until the next day. They knew I had to stay overnight, so they asked us to call them when we were notified that Joey was awake. Then my parents left. Kyle stayed.

Kyle stayed all night. The nurses brought us water and iced tea (which was horrible because it was flat hospital iced tea). In the middle of the night, Kyle turned on the television and flipped through the channels. We were provided extra pillows so Kyle was able to prop himself up on pillows next to me rather than have his head against the headboard. We ended up watching old episodes of Seinfeld, and somehow they were able to make me laugh.

Eventually, as the sun was rising, we both fell asleep and were out for a couple of hours. We were awakened by a doctor coming in to tell me that I needed to follow up with my primary care physician within the week. He gave me a prescription of several medications and told me to drink water and Gatorades to help with hydration. I was being released.

Kyle asked about Joey. The doctor said that Joey was not his patient, but he knew that Joey had woken up about twenty minutes ago.

I told Kyle to hurry to Joey and that I would meet him there as soon as I was unhooked from the IVs and formally discharged. He left, and the nurses came into the room and helped me dress into my own clothes and stand up to walk. My legs felt wobbly, but they worked. I thanked them and moved to leave. One nurse insisted on wheeling me in a wheelchair, which would have been fine, except that she did not have one on hand. She forced me to wait on the bed until she returned. It took far too long, and my impatience got the best of me. I pushed the nurse's button and told them I was going to my brother's room.

Joey looked terrible. He had tubes coming out of his nose, his mouth, his arms, and his stomach. He could not talk because of the tubes down his throat. He tried to smile, but he could hardly move his face. Kyle told me he had seen the doctor, who told him that Joey would be able to talk and have most of the tubes removed by the end of the day.

I rubbed my brother's arm and told him that we were glad he was all right and that we had missed him while he was in surgery. Joey did not know that I was admitted for dehydration, and he certainly did not know that the surgery indicated he would be dead within the year. Right now, he just needed to regain his strength from the surgery.

"I love you, Joey," I said.

"I actually love you more than she does," Kyle said with a halfhearted grin.

This made Joey's face move. It would have been a smile if he was not stuffed full of tubes.

Kyle started talking to Joey about my embarrassing passing out and subsequent vomiting. While he made light of my mortifying episode, I called my parents to tell them Joey was awake. I walked out of the room as I talked, and I warned my parents about how bad he looked. I reminded them that he did not yet know his prognosis, so it would be best if we said nothing until he had some of his strength back.

Both my mom and dad arrived in record time. As soon as they came into the room, I left to grab breakfast. While I was out, I stopped by my parents' house. A shower and a fresh change of clothes helped me feel much better. On my way out, I grabbed some of Joey's clothes and some toiletries for Kyle in case he wanted to shower in Joey's room.

I returned to the hospital an hour later and distributed the Starbucks treats and handed Kyle the bag I brought for him. The tube was out of Joey's mouth and there was a smaller tube in his nose. He had more color in his face than when I left. I walked over to him and kissed his cheek. "You look so much better in just the short time I was gone," I softly said to him.

My brother whispered, "I can't believe you didn't bring me Starbucks."

I smiled at him, and at the fact that he had not lost his spirit.

My brother's doctor came into the room and asked Joey how he was feeling. Joey half smiled and whispered that he was in a lot of pain. He had also been gagging a lot and his stomach was cramping. The doctor said they would increase his pain medication and that the cramping should subside as the hours passed.

Then the doctor explained to Joey what was discovered during surgery. He said that in the next few days, Joey would have to decide what treatment he wanted, if any. But the doctor made it clear that the treatment would only prolong his life by a few months. No treatment would cure him.

We all knew this information already, but it still felt as shocking and painful to me as if it was the first time. Some stupid part of me had hoped the doctor would say that Joey would live and the cancer was nothing more than a brief scare. Hearing it again was just confirmation of the inevitable.

Joey did not respond. After the doctors excused themselves, he held out his hand for my mom. He looked to her and whispered that he was sorry, and she dissolved into tears.

"Don't be sorry, baby. *I* am sorry. I'm so, so, so sorry. We're just going to pray about this. Okay? Joey, we're going to pray about this." The tears were flowing down her face before she could attempt to hold them back.

Kyle walked over to me and held my hand. My dad sat on the bed next to my brother and reassured Joey that he would make it through this. "We are going to look at our options and fight this together, as a family."

Dad said that he wanted to pray. We gathered around the bed, and my father prayed that God's will would be done. That was it. He prayed that God would heal his son and spare Joey from any pain and suffering. "God, we worship you and know that everything is for your glory. We trust you and your plan even if it is not our plan. But we beg for your mercy and healing on my son. Amen."

We stayed there with our hands on Joey for a long moment. Eventually, as we all settled down again, Joey's eyes began to close. My mother told us that Joey needed to sleep and that she would stay with him. My dad needed to run errands for magazines and books to bring back to the hospital. I wanted to go home and take a nap. Kyle offered to drive me.

Kyle drove me to my parents' house. We were both so emotionally exhausted that neither one of us said anything. When we parked in the driveway, I thanked him for the ride.

He said, "Call me when you're awake, please. I want to come check on you. I'll bring you some Gatorade, and I'll fill your prescriptions and bring them too."

"I promise to call you. Thank you, Kyle. For everything." I leaned over and kissed his cheek. I got out of his car and went straight to bed.

15

I brought my laptop and a box of work to the hospital. I balanced my iced tea between the box and my bag as I entered Joey's recovery room. He was sitting up watching television. He still had an IV in his arm and the tube on his side, but his face was cleared of all wires, and he grinned when he saw me. Joey could not move too much, but his face could shine again.

I placed my materials on the moving tray before I gave my brother a soft hug. I held his hand and asked him how he was feeling. In slightly louder than a whisper, he said, "My stomach hurts, but I'm feeling better by the minute."

"Always optimistic," I responded, squeezing his hand. "Do you mind if I set up my office in here and keep you company?"

"Not if you don't mind regular interruptions by nurses and visitors," he jibed as loud as he could.

"Not a problem," I said as I took out my laptop and a few files. I sat in the chair in the corner of the room and moved the rolling tray to my corner. It didn't take me look to become fully engrossed in my emails and messages. The FDA had previously approved of Venergy, but they were still requiring certain documentation. I had been sent an email asserting they had all the information and documents needed and the approval stood for Venergy. I had three hundred contacts from major buyers come to me in the past week. Darren and David had sent an email asking if we should hire someone to address the individual sales of Venergy now that people were constantly calling to ask for it. My product was a huge success, and, to be frank, I was excited.

I looked up at my brother, who was still sitting up in the bed—well, the bed was sitting up and he was leaning against it. His eyes were closing while he watched television. I thought about how he would not need the vitamin anymore. My heart sank at the thought of his body just slowly deteriorating, how there was nothing any of us could do about it.

After a moment, I heard, "Quit staring at me and work."

I snorted and went back to my emails. The shareholder meeting on Molly was at the end of the week, and I had at least fifty messages from shareholders and members of the Board asking me questions in preparation of that meeting. It would likely be the most attended shareholder meeting in years. I had my file on Molly, and I planned on preparing that presentation while in the hospital, going to work on Thursday for copies and to set up for the meeting, then presenting on Friday. After that, I could return home Friday afternoon.

I pulled photographs of children who were sick with the leukemia from the internet. I saved interviews of parents who lost children to the disease, and I researched information on Ecstasy and the truth of its effects. I would use the presentation I had given to the Board, but I was going to remake it into something more emotional, more personal.

I was confident I could get the required number of votes from the shareholders. I knew, from my meetings with the original Molly scientist, that I could get a fair contract with him for the drug. I had already begun completing the application and paperwork for FDA approval, and I planned on sending a request for an in-person meeting with someone from the FDA to discuss the drug. I knew people who knew people—I was going to make it happen.

As I was returning various emails to Sandy, my parents barged into the room with bags of food in their hands. I looked up from my computer to greet them. My mom was shoving a straw in my brother's mouth, begging him to drink the Ensure she brought for him. She insisted he needed to eat. My dad instantly grabbed the remote control and started looking for the news.

"Mom, you know he might not be allowed to drink yet," I piped up. "You should maybe ask a nurse before you mess up his stomach and make him worse."

"Go back to your work, Miss Know-It-All. I'll ask a nurse, and then he will drink this." She turned to my dad. "Honey, give me the remote."

"Why?"

"I want to call the nurse."

"Just go out there and get her yourself." He did not stop flipping the channels or turn around and look at her.

"Just give it to me, for crying out loud!" Mom yanked it out of his hand and pushed the "call nurse" button. My father smiled when he noticed the channel-flipping had stopped on a news station.

"Yes?" a voice sounded from the remote.

"Hi, this is Joey's mom. Can he drink Ensure? I brought it in for him. It is full of nutrients, and he needs to eat." I resisted the urge to sigh as she explained herself.

"No, sorry," the nurse replied. "He cannot take anything by mouth yet. He can have a piece of ice to suck on if his mouth gets dry, but nothing else."

My mom turned to me, her face pinched up. She hated being told no, but more than that, she hated being wrong. "Are you happy, smarty-pants?" she asked, as if I was the one who had told her no.

I shook my head and returned to working. Dad watched the news, and Mom plopped down next to Joey, rubbing his arm and talking to him. After about half an hour of peace and quiet, a barrage of nurses came in to check Joey's tubes, his bedding, and God knows what else. My mom and dad left the room until the nurses were finished. I turned toward the window, put in my earbuds, and kept working.

There was a Board member in MedVasive who was a great salesman, but we had been having trouble with him. I was reviewing his personnel file via email and evaluating how we should handle certain situations with him, including his sale techniques and some untoward allegations brought against him. Sandy texted me that he was a pig and should be fired—I sent back a smiley face while continuing to review his file.

Once I was finished, I wrote to the Double Ds my recommendation of what to do with him. Halfway through the recommendation, I felt a hand on my shoulder, and I nearly jumped out of my skin. I turned around, tugging out my earbuds, to see Kyle was standing over me.

Joey had been completely changed into regular clothes, though the same tubing was attached to him. My dad was watching the news again, and my mom was reading a magazine while sitting on my brother's bed. I had gotten so involved in my work that I did not even realize the nurses were done, my parents were back, and we had a visitor.

He was wearing his work clothes and he smelled like musky pine. I took in a deep breath to enjoy the smell. "I just stopped by on my way to work to see how he was doing and to check on you," he said. "How are you feeling?"

I smiled at his consideration. "I think I'm back to normal. Well, my normal, anyway."

Kyle commented that he knew I must have slept a long time because he kept calling my parents' house to check on me, and they kept telling him I was still sleeping. "Oh, and I'm going to have to ask you for more Venergy stock. My customers are buying it all as soon as I put it out. I actually started taking it myself. Can you tell?" he asked while flexing his bicep.

"No," I laughed as I squeezed his arm. I promised to get him extra shipments of the vitamin by the end of the day. He said he planned to return to the hospital after his shift, and he asked me to call him if anything happened. Then Kyle walked over to Joey, placed his hand on the top of my brother's head, and smiled at him.

"Bye, buddy," he said. Joey smiled back, but that was all before Kyle left the room. He seemed to be growing more lethargic than he was when I arrived earlier in the day.

After another few hours of working, a doctor came into the room and talked to us about more results that had come in about Joey's condition. "He's doing exceptionally well. He should be able to go home with nursing care by Thursday. But the lab results have come back, and the cancer seems to be very aggressive, as we suspected. Actually, we haven't seen many cancers this aggressive before. We don't want to have to wait on the chemotherapy. We plan to implant a port in his right shoulder so we can begin chemotherapy through it. This, of course, is an option. We will not force you into any kind of treatment."

My mom's lips were tight. "What would you do if it was your son?" she asked.

The doctor said he would go with the plan as he set forth, so my parents and Joey agreed to it. The port would be inserted the next day, and chemotherapy would be started on the weekend. The doctor promised that, by the end of the day, he would make sure we received material on the type of cancer my brother had, as well as detailed information on the treatment he would be receiving.

My dad spoke up. "What caused him to get this?"

The doctor bowed his head and admitted that they had no idea. They had not seen this specific type of cancer act so violently so quickly before, even though they had treated many cases of esophageal cancer in many patients. "It's somewhat of a mystery to our entire oncology team. We're submitting samples and information to cancer research facilities to try to determine the cause."

The air seemed to be sucked out of the room when the doctor left and closed the door behind him. No one said a word for several minutes, nor did anyone move. After some time, my mom asked my brother if he wanted some Ensure. In unison, my father and I said, "He can't have anything…"

I grabbed my phone and walked over to Joey, lifted his hand, and kissed it. I told him I would be back in a few moments and not to let Mom and Dad drive him crazy. Then I walked out of the room toward the hospital exit—along the way, I concentrated on keeping my breaths long and calming.

When I stepped out of the sliding doors, I called Sandy. I updated her on my brother and my plan for working for the next few months both remotely and at the office. Sandy was kind about Joey, and she let me in on what was going on back at MedVasive. I told her I would be there in two days and we could address any issues then.

I hung up and called Kyle next. When he answered, he was in the middle of working with a customer, and he had a line of people waiting for their prescriptions. I immediately felt flushes and intrusive. "Hey, I have an update from Joey's doctor. I just wanted to call and tell you. Sorry I caught you at a bad time. Yo can call me later."

"Uh, no, just a second," Kyle responded. I heard him call over an employee to check out the people in line, and then there were a few seconds of silence. "Okay," he said. "I'm free. Kat, you there?"

"Yeah, I'm here." I told him all that the doctor had said about Joey's cancer. I told him my plans for work and my parents' plans for staying with my brother. In a quiet voice, Kyle said he would come to the hospital as soon as he was off of work, and he would do all he could to help Joey and our family. He apologized for the horrible situation, and he let me go so he could return to helping his customers.

I stood outside for a long while, Kyle's gentle, strong voice remaining in my head. Eventually, I had to remind myself that he was engaged before my thoughts got away from me. I turned tail and hurried back inside—for the rest of the day, I immersed myself in spending time with my brother and working, and then took my turn sleeping at the hospital in the uncomfortable pleather foldout chair.

16

I stood before the Board members and shareholders for the final vote on Molly. The conference table was full, and there were chairs that lined the walls. There were so many people in the room that at least forty of those attending were forced to stand because there were no more chairs available.

I wore a conservative suit, my hair pulled back in a lazy half-ponytail, and the black rings around my eyes were the makeup of sheer exhaustion. Sandy was standing next to me, as perky as ever, with a laptop on a podium. She would be in charge of the slides on the on-screen presentation while I spoke.

The lights dimmed, and the room grew completely silent despite the multitude of people packed inside.

Sandy lit up the first slide. It was a photograph of a bald

child with a pale face, stick limbs, and a forced smile. "Brittany is three years old," I began. "She was diagnosed with acute leukemia at only four months. Since her diagnosis, Brittany has had several blood transfusions, spent over four-hundred days in the hospital, lost her hair, suffered through three rounds of strong chemotherapy, and she is currently getting radiation once a week. Brittany cannot eat without getting sick and has to use a feeding tube to keep her body functioning."

The next slide popped up. It was a picture of Brittany's parents talking to the doctor. The mother's expression required no explanation. Grasping at the father was an eight year old boy. His face was completely buried in his father's leg, and the man had his hand on the little boy's back.

"The family's pediatric oncologist is explaining to the parents that Brittany can try another round of the chemotherapy, in all but likelihood, it will be too hard on her body and could kill her. Their best option is to just continue with the pain medication regimen and enjoy their last few months with their daughter."

I then explained child leukemia to my audience, the statistics of children who suffered from the disease, and the number of kids each year who died. I told them that we had in our hands a vaccine that could keep others from suffering like Brittany and her family. The vaccine would be optional, and would be optimal when given to a child between the ages of six months and a year. Sandy kept up with me, flipping through slides that provided written and photographic information coinciding with my speech.

Then I paused, and I allowed myself, and the room, to

breathe. A moment later, I looked at Sandy and nodded. She switched to the next slide, which showed a graphic of a teenager in a dance club, chasing down a pill with a beer. The word ECSTACY was written across the top of the slide

Scattered gasps filled the room, and people started to mumble. I waited a few seconds, allowed them their initial reactions, and then I explained the one negative to the vaccine and the manner in which it could be perceived.

"Ladies and gentlemen, an element of Ecstasy is part of this vaccine. However, despite what you may think, it is actually less poisonous and less toxic than chemotherapy. Only three percent of the vaccine is made up of the Ecstasy element, and tests have shown that I will not in any way affect the children who are given the vaccination. But this picture, this slide, *this* is what the media will show. They will likely accuse MedVasive of promoting the injection of an illegal drug in infants. Debates will be made over where the Ecstasy elements will originate and the possibility of the drug being used by others. If one child dies or gets ill from the vaccine, the Ecstasy will immediately be blamed. If one of the children who receive the vaccine grows up and becomes addicted to Ecstasy, the media could blame the vaccine as the cause of his or her dependence. This is a serious issue that we need to discuss in detail and carefully approach with the media if we take on this drug."

The shareholders began talking to each other in earnest, and everyone seemed to stop listening to me. I looked at Sandy and rolled my hand, indicating for her to go to the next slide. The new slide was the photograph of the little girl with

101

leukemia, Brittany. The slide spanned out, and instead of just Brittany, there were at least twenty faces of children with the disease. The image continued to expand until it was hundreds, then thousands, then too many faces to make out. I listened to the voices in the room grow quiet as more eyes turned back to the screen, to the image.

"I know this is risky for the company," I said. "I understand this will cause a lot of controversy. But I think we can do this. MedVasive has a reputation of being trustworthy and honest. If any company can succeed at promoting a vaccine that cures leukemia with an element of Ecstasy, it's us. This is a company that all of you in here built for the purpose of killing diseases and helping people. There are kids we can save. We can prevent the heartache of the families who watch their young children suffer and die. MedVasive can handle the controversy, and I vow to be on the front line and take full responsibility for the inclusion of the Ecstasy element. I will fight for the people's trust until everyone is asking their pediatricians for it."

I could tell by their reactions that I almost had them. I was almost there. I added a final push to get what I wanted. "If this blows up in our faces and the media slaughters MedVasive, I will personally take the blame, and you may do what you will with me publicly. I will be the fall man, and you can change the focus to Venergy and its extreme success to date."

A few moments of silence. Then, Darren and David stood from their seats and walked to my sides. They both announced that they were voting for MedVasive to produce the vaccine, and they supported me all the way. Darren then asked for a vote.

The votes were written on slips prepared by Sandy and gathered by her in a large box. While Sandy collected the boxes, I promptly gathered my materials and left the room. I went straight to my office, shut the door behind me, dropped everything on my desk, and fell back onto my couch with a long, loud breath. I sat in the quiet. It took everything I had to try to convince myself that, even if I didn't get the votes, life would go on.

Interrupting my silence, Sandy and the Double Ds entered my office without knocking. I didn't bother to turn and look at them. "So?" I asked.

Sandy said that the shareholders were still in the conference room, and they were asking for me. To this, I craned my head to look at her. "Why?"

Darren walked over and held out his hand, and I allowed him to pull me to my feet. I groaned at the thought of having to go back into the conference room, but we all left my office anyway. Inside the room, everyone was up and mingling. When they saw me, conversations stopped in their tracks, and there was a beat before they all began asking me questions about how long it would take to get the drug on the market, how much the cost-profit would be. The votes had passed, and the shareholders now wanted more information about timelines, FDA approval, and marketing strategies.

I answered all of the questions, while periodically looking at the Double Ds in confusion. At one point, Sandy leaned over and whispered in my ear that there had been only one vote against Molly. I was so shocked that one shareholder had to ask me his question twice before I realized he was talking to me.

After an hour of discussion, I managed to explain to the group that I had another meeting waiting for me. I thanked them for their support and promised to dedicate my all to Molly's launch. I was so very happy that the drug had passed so relieved, that, on my way out of the conference room, I nearly started to cry.

Once the crowd had finally dispersed, Sandy came to my office to find me. She found me curled up on my couch, my face wet with tears. Softly, my assistant lifted me to my feet. She grabbed my purse and my iced tea. "Go home," she said. "Go to spin class. Go spend the rest of the day sleeping. Just do whatever. You need a mini vacation from life, and you deserve it."

I told her she couldn't give me orders, and she laughed. I took my purse and tea from her and headed to the elevators. I passed Judy, the snobby receptionist, without a word. As I entered the elevator, the receptionist smirked down the hall at me and said, "Way to go, Ms. MedVasive."

That made me smile. During the ride to the first floor, I thought about what I wanted to do. I longed to sleep, but I knew that was just the stress and anxiety. I had already worked out that morning, so I did not really need to go running. The elevator dinged and the doors slid open, but the ding felt like it came from inside me, like a lightbulb turning on. I knew what I wanted to do.

I stepped out of the elevator, pulled my phone out of new Louis Vuitton bag, and pushed Kyle's speed dial. The phone rang twice, and then he answered. I froze. I stopped walking in the middle of the lobby of the building. I had not even considered what I would say if he answered.

"Hey, Kat." He laughed when I said nothing. "I know it's you."

I blinked out of my trance. "Kyle, hey. Sorry. I got distracted for a second." Kyle said that he could tell, and he asked if something was wrong. "No, no. That's not why I called."

"Why did you call, Kat?"

That left me speechless—I realized I wasn't entirely sure why.

"Um, well… I had a huge meeting that just finished up, and I'm done with work for the day, and, well, um, I thought maybe you would want to drive to Sarasota. Maybe go kayaking, and dinner, or something. But you're probably working, and it's a long drive. You know, Janet probably wouldn't like it, so never mind. Forget it. Sorry. I'm a mess. Pretend this never happened. I'm hanging up now." I was mortified. What was I thinking, just randomly calling him?

"Kat! Kat, wait. Don't hang up. It's okay. I don't have to work today or tomorrow, and I don't mind the drive. And you don't have to worry about Janet." He went quiet for a moment before he added, "I broke up with her."

My jaw dropped.

"Okay…" I cleared my throat and tried again. "Okay, great. I guess I'll see you in about two hours. I'll have the kayaks ready by the time you get there. Drive safe." I hung up and ran out of the building.

17

I ran around my home like a madwoman, picking up clothes and dusting everything. I lit a candle in virtually every room and cleared the dishes from the kitchen. Then, I jumped in the shower and dressed casual as if I had just thrown something together last minute. I fixed my hair into the perfect ponytail and put on just enough make up to seem like most of it wore off but in the most beautiful way possible. I was completely ready for my company with thirty minutes to spare. It was the absolute longest thirty minutes of my life. I paced, I tried to read but could not concentrate, I reviewed work emails but found I was entirely too enthusiastic in my responses.

Finally, I called Sandy. "What do you think I should do when he gets here?" I pressed her as I paced around my house. "I mean, should I invite him in? Would that be too forward?

But he might need to use the bathroom after the trip. Should I wear my purple or silver bikini when we kayak? I don't know if we should eat first or after kayaking. Should I offer him—?"

Sandy interrupted me with a laugh. "Kathy, slow down. I'm pretty sure he wouldn't come all this way if he didn't feel for you the way you feel for him. Just relax and enjoy your time with him."

"I'm *nervous*, Sandy. I don't know how to act or what to say. I'm going to ruin it because I'm such a mess."

"Okay, well, pretend you two are in college. Pretend you guys are visiting from school for a holiday. Don't be in today. Pretend to be in yesterday, before life got complicated."

I took in a deep breath. I thanked Sandy, and we hung up our call. Finally, I sat down, and I thought back on when I was in law school, when I would visit my family for holidays. I thought about when Kyle would walk through the door after his drive from pharmacy school, how my entire family would light up at the sight of him.

The doorbell rang, and I was thrown back into reality. I dropped my phone on the kitchen bar and answered the door. Kyle was there, in khaki shorts, an untucked red polo shirt, and loafers. He smiled and rubbed his hair. I smiled back, and neither of us said a word. Then, when it became slightly awkward, I moved out of the way and asked him to come in.

Kyle had never visited before, so I gave him the grand tour. He complimented my setup before he asked to use the bathroom. Once I showed him where it was, I ran to my room and changed into my purple bathing suit, over which I threw a sheer, form-fitting wrap. Kyle was in the living room when

I came back out. He was looking out of my back glass doors, which overlooked the water. The two kayaks were leaning against a tree near the shore.

"Ready?" I asked as I grabbed two cold water bottles out of the refrigerator. I tossed him one and opened the sliding glass door. Without responding, Kyle followed me out.

We walked across my yard and pulled the kayaks across the grass, through the rocks and shallow water. It was afternoon and the sun was shining directly over us, making the surface of the ocean shimmer. I took off my wrap and threw it on the front of the kayak. Kyle also shed his shirt and was left in just his khaki shorts. I turned on Pandora on my phone, which I had in a special waterproof covering; I had a speaker receptor in Kyle's kayak, which would allow us both to enjoy the music as we cruised across the water. We headed down the beautiful blue waters of the Gulf, padding right, left, right, left, virtually in unison.

From that moment forward, Kyle and I let the conversation flow between his pharmacy, Venergy, our small home town, and what music we had been into recently. We never spoke of my brother or Janet. After an hour of nonstop kayaking, we reached a sandbar close to a stretch of the beach. When it was too shallow to paddle, we stepped out into the water and walked our kayaks to the beach. We pulled them all the way out of the water, then stretched out on our backs on the white sand. The music played soft and sweet as we watched the waves crash over the shore and trickle to our feet.

The sun was bright on our faces. After a few moments of letting my muscles rest, I pulled myself onto my elbows and looked around the beach. There were some families playing in the water, a few kids making sand castles, and a woman lounging in a chair with a book. In the far distance was a couple running down the edge of the beach. It was a weekday, so the shoreline was fairly empty.

Before lying back down, I looked at Kyle next to me. He had an arm draped over his eyes and the other over his stomach, lying still and breathing deep. I couldn't look away from him. This man, he was home to me. I could not imagine my life without him.

I shifted down into the sand and tried to drag my thoughts away to something else when I considered what I would have done had he married Janet. *Pretend we're in a time before Janet and cancer and careers*, I reminded myself.

Kyle rolled toward me and propped himself up on one elbow. I mimicked him so we faced each other. He smirked and asked, "Do you remember when we were in high school and your brother fell asleep, so we took all of rolls of toilet paper from your house and filled his room with little pieces of toilet paper?"

I laughed out. "Of course I remember. I also remember cleaning it all up by myself as punishment from my mom!" I scrunched my nose.

"Do you remember my freshman homecoming?" I asked, and Kyle made a sad face in response.

"Aw, yes. You poor thing."

We both laughed. "I was so excited," I reminisced. "It took me *weeks* to find my dress. I got my hair professionally done and everything."

"And that jerk never showed up. You waited over an hour before you finally gave up on him."

"What a loser. Why would anyone do that?" I responded. "But you and Joey were at the dance with two girls."

"Sara and Anna," Kyle said. "Your dad showed up and told us what happened, and we went back with him to your house."

"You totally ditched Sara," I needled him.

"I did," he groaned. Then he laughed. "But we got back to your house, and I saw you before your mom cleaned you up. Your face was a *mess*." He got quieter. "But you were beautiful, even back then."

I didn't speak for a few seconds. "That was a disaster. Well, sort of. Well, actually, not really. I got to go back to the dance with you. I mean, but still, it wasn't that great." The moment the words were out of my mouth, I was embarrassed.

"What do you mean, 'it wasn't that great'?" Kyle teased. "You make it sound like you had a terrible time with me." He drew himself closer to me. I lay on my back to give him room, and he was propped so close that he blocked the sun from my eyes.

"I wanted you to be my date because you chose me" I murmured, "not because you were rescuing me from a jerk who stood me up." I diverted my eyes away from him as I spoke. "I mean, I had fun when we danced and played around with our friends. But when we were slow dancing, I remember looking at all the real couples and wishing you would hold me the way they were holding each other. But, you know, kids—we were just kids."

Kyle just watched me. I raised my eyes to meet his. "Your

parents were so good to me when I was younger," he said. "They took me in and treated me like their own son. I had no real family, and they made me feel like I was part of theirs. Even now, they still feel like the parents I never really knew."

Kyle seemed to be confiding some deep secret, but it wasn't something that I didn't already know. I only stayed silent as he continued. "At that dance, I wanted to tell you there was no other girl in that room I would have rather been with. I thought that when I went to pharmacy school, I would find someone, that I would move on—but no one ever came close to you. But...for some reason, I thought I would be betraying your parents if I dated their daughter. Like, we basically lived in the same home. I felt weird about doing that to them."

All I could do was shake my head. "What about now? What about the last few years? Did your feelings change?"

Kyle moved back away from me, releasing the sunlight into my eyes. "I felt like after you went to law school, you moved on from your old life. You were more than this town. You were more than a guy who was just a pharmacist. My feelings didn't matter anymore."

I sat up and wrapped my arms around my legs, scrunching the sand beneath my toes. The waves crashed, and children screamed and laughed in the distance. "I am not too good for you, Kyle, and I never will be. I will always be that girl you danced with, and you're always going to be the guy I want to take me to that dance."

Kyle watched me, his eyes careful as they scanned my face. He then brought his hand around the back of my neck and pulled me close before he brought his lips to mine in a hard kiss, a kiss I had waited years for. His sandy hands cupped my face, and then he pulled away and pressed our foreheads together. He took a breath and chuckled. "Kat, Kat, Kat." I just smiled.

He kissed me softly again, and again, and I lost track of time. At some point, he lay back, and I rested against him. He rubbed my back as I rested my head on his chest. "I love you," he said, as if he was commenting on the weather.

"I love you too," I murmured against his skin. "I always have."

"Can I tell you something?" he asked. I said yes, of course. "I never really liked Janet." He went on to tell me about how he could have cared for Janet in a respectable way, and he could have had a family with her the way he always wanted, but he always would have loved me. He never could have gone through with it.

The sun was nearing the horizon, and I realized we would have to rush to make it back before dark. I helped Kyle to his feet and dragged him back to the water's edge. We pushed our kayaks into the water, jumped in, and started paddling. We raced each other on the way back as we tried to beat the sun. By the light of the moon, we pulled the kayaks into the yard behind my house, and we ran inside laughing, adrenaline still pumping through our veins.

I gave Kyle permission to slip away for a quick shower, and I made us some smoothies while I waited for him. He was out of the shower and donning a different pair of khakis and a blue polo within minutes, and we settled down at the kitchen bar to drink our smoothies. We agreed to tell my parents and

Joey that we were a couple, and that we would both meet with them that coming weekend, when I was visiting, so we could tell them together.

Once we were finished with our smoothies, I slid out of my seat and put our cups in the sink. Kyle followed, and he wrapped his arms around me and kissed the crook of my neck. He promised to call later this week, and he told me he loved me. A few moments later, I stood against my red door while I watched him drive away, and I could hardly believe how quickly my life had changed in one evening.

I floated into work the next day. I contacted the scientist who had initially brought Molly to us, and I started contract negotiations for the new vaccine. Afterward, I sent a letter to the company director, officers, and shareholders, congratulating them on the FDA approval of Venergy and on the start of the negotiations for the purchase of Molly. I confirmed the date of my Dr. Oz reappearance in a few weeks with those in charge, and got the chance to speak with the stylists who would be taking care of me. I worked long hours all until Friday, and then I left for Dade City. I drove the entire way with a smile.

18

The moment I reached my parents' house, I ran straight to the restroom.

I yelled hello to my mother as I passed her in the kitchen, and I patted my father's head when I rushed behind the couch where he sat watching television. When I finished cleaning up, I rejoined my parents, first leaning over to kiss my dad's cheek. He patted my hand, but his usual enthusiasm was gone. I joined my mom, who was busy cooking. I asked her what I could do to help, and she told me to cook the peas and corn. I did as I was told, but I felt a heaviness in the room that I couldn't shake.

As I opened the frozen bag of peas, I snuck a glance at Mom's face. She was pale. She looked thinner than the last time I had seen her, and her eyes seemed swollen.

I filled the pot with water before I decided to ask how Joey was doing. I assumed he was out of the house since I had not seen him when I arrived. My mother stopped what she was doing. She did not look at me. She did not move.

"He's having a hard time," she said tightly. "He can't eat without throwing up. He's in a lot of pain, and we have to take him to the emergency room for IV fluids at least every other day."

I stared at her. "What? Mom, why didn't you tell me any of this?"

She sighed. "Every time I talk to you on the phone, you seem so happy. I didn't want to bring you down. There was nothing you could do in Sarasota but worry anyway." Then she slid down to the floor and rested her back against the cabinet. I sat next to her, pressing up against her side.

"How are *you* doing?" I asked. "How are you holding up?" I placed my hand on her leg.

My mom said that she was tired. She was sad, and numb. "Wait until you have children. There's nothing worse than watching your baby suffer and knowing there's nothing you can do. The worst part is the doctor told us Joey will not get better. We have to keep making decisions about chemotherapy and radiation and pain medications…"

Her voice trailed off. She rested her head on my shoulder, and I felt her tears dampen my shirt sleeve. I put my hands around her hands, and silently, I prayed. I prayed for us, for my brother, and for God's peace that passed all understanding. We just sat there, without movement or talking.

After what must have been about five minutes, we were

interrupted by a knock at the door. I heard Kyle's muffled voice letting us know he was coming into the house. He didn't see us on the kitchen floor, so he went straight to the living room where my dad sat.

"Mom, I thought Joey was out with Kyle." She simply shook her head. I stood up, reached out my hand, and pulled her to her feet. I took a moment to put the corn and peas on the stove before I hurried to find Joey.

The inside of his bedroom was dark when I stepped inside, and it smelled like a stomach-churning mix of vomit and chicken noodle soup. It took a few seconds for my eyes to adjust to the lack of light. Once I could see, I spotted my brother in his bed, curled up in a ball under a blanket. He was facing me with his eyes open and staring at nothing. There was a bowl of soup on the bedside table next to a glass of ice water, and an empty bucket sat next to the bed.

"Hey there," I whispered as I crept over to his bed and sat next to him. I put my hand on his head, my fingers stroking his hair as I asked him how he was doing. In a weak voice, he said he wasn't feeling that great, but he was better now that I was around.

I heard footsteps in the hall, and then Kyle say, "Hey, man," from the doorway. He walked in, turned over the empty vomit bucket, and sat next to the bed. He and I gave each other a look of concern. "I heard you're having a hard time." He placed his hand on Joey's shoulder. "Anything I can do?"

My brother merely shook his head.

The room was so dark. "Joey, you want to move into the living room and get out some movies?" I asked. "You need new smells and new blankets and people around you. Can we do that?" Kyle piped in that, as a pharmacist, he thought it would be the perfect medicine.

I jumped up and ran to the living room. I asked my dad to move over to the plush recliner, and then I grabbed a sheet and spread it over the couch. I pulled our fluffiest pillows out of the back bedroom and opened up all of the curtains. Kyle came in with his arm around Joey, helping him walk to the couch. I tucked a soft brown throw blanket around my brother when he was settled in. Kyle picked up the remote and started flipping through the channels to find something he knew Joey would like.

My mother came in from the kitchen and she sat at the foot of the couch, placing Joey's feet on her lap. As they all gravitated around him, I went back to Joey's room and pulled off the sheets and comforter and dirty clothes, then threw them all in the washing machine. I opened Joey's window and started dusting and scrubbing off everything in his dank, smelly room. Alone in the room, trying as best I could to make the place feel clean again, I couldn't help but cry.

I kept seeing Joey's pale, sunken face in my mind. He seemed to have aged thirty years since I had last seen him, and his body had lost so much weight that his limbs looked like bones with thin skin wrapped around them. Hearing how bad he was doing from my mom had been hard, but seeing him was like a punch to the chest.

When I had scrubbed and dusted until my hands ached, I dug around in the kitchen until I found an old candle. I lit it and brought it to my brother's room to chase out the stale smells. Once I was satisfied with my work, I slipped into the bathroom to clean my face of my tears. As I was washing up, I noticed the bathtub. I turned around and, for a moment, I just stared at it.

I returned to the living room and asked Kyle and my dad to help Joey to the bathtub. My brother curled further into the couch and protested that he did not want a bath. He was clearly embarrassed by his state, and Dad and Kyle, clearly unsure of what to do, looked at me.

"Joey, just a quick wash. You'll feel so much better, I promise," I pleaded with him. Joey said nothing in reply, but he allowed himself to be assisted to the bathroom by Kyle and my dad. Mom grabbed clean clothes and a towel and set them on the counter next to the tub before allowing the men their privacy. When she joined me out in the empty kitchen, I embraced her in a hug that only a mother and a sister of a dying boy could share.

The men returned to the living room a little less than half an hour later. Joey had a touch more color in his cheeks, and what little hair he still had was damp. He was in clean clothes and set up on a clean couch. Kyle flopped down next to him and managed to find one of those crazy obstacle course competition shows that always made my brother laugh. My mom returned to the foot of the couch with Joey's feet on her lap, my dad in the recliner. I sat on the other side of the couch next to Kyle.

As we watched the show, Kyle's hand sneaked between us to lace his fingers with mine. His touch made me feel safe, and it gave me the comfort I needed to breathe easier. Kyle was watching his best friend die and doing the best he could to make things better, but he still thought to take the time to show me comfort. I loved him for it.

The commentators were making fun of the show contestants, giving them nicknames and making all sorts of silly puns. Joey giggled as one guy flew through the air and landed against a huge foam wall, and I could feel the mood of the entire room lift at his happiness. It was well past time to eat dinner, but Mom had turned off the stove during Joey's bath, and none of us made the move to mention food.

Joey attempted to sit up against the pillows, and my mother and I both jumped to tuck additional pillows behind him so he would be comfortable. "Are you feeling better, sweetheart?" my mom asked as she helped him position himself.

"Yeah, actually, I feel a little better. I almost feel hungry."

"Can I get you anything?" I asked.

"My guitar?" he responded hesitantly.

With a smile, I went to his room and retrieved his guitar. My father muted the TV as I handed the instrument to my brother. He did not seem to feel well enough to sing, but he could still play. I closed my eyes and enjoyed the sound of "Amazing Grace" flowing from Joey's strumming fingers. He began to whisper the verses, and as the seconds passed, we all joined in, strengthening his too-quiet voice with our own.

I prayed that God would never let me forget this moment. I wanted to imprint it in my mind so that the memory would never fade, to give it its own space where it would remain untouched for the rest of my life. When the song was over, Joey just kept strumming chords.

While he played a medley, he looked at Kyle. "How is Janet?" he asked. "We haven't talked about the wedding in a while."

Kyle looked at me, and I just shrugged. Joey stopped strumming, and the room was silent. The more time that passed without an answer, the more my family's attention on Kyle seemed to sharpen.

"Well, um," he finally explained, "I broke up with Janet. It turns out she was never right for me. I don't think I ever really loved her." Kyle then apologized to my mother for the work she had put into the engagement party for a wedding that was not happening.

After the initial startled surprise wore off, my dad leaned in and gave Kyle a thoughtful look. "What made you change your mind?"

Kyle's face flushed red, and for a second, I thought he might need Joey's vomit bucket. I decided to cut him a break.

"Well, see, Kyle and I are dating." I said simply, nothing more. I just raised my eyebrows and hunched my shoulders in a "*what do you think?*" gesture.

I didn't expect Joey to start smiling, so big that it creased his face and his watery eyes. "God is so good to me," he whispered.

Overcome with relief, I got up and hugged my brother. Kyle joined me, and my mom, sitting in the middle of us, put a gentle hand on Joey's face. My dad came over and knelt next to us, his hands wrapped around his children.

After a moment of quiet, I heard Joey say, "I think I want to try eating now." We all laughed, and the embrace broke apart. My mother and I turned the living room into a dining room and served everyone the dishes she had been preparing earlier. Joey ate a small bite of the peas and corn, but nothing more. He then had to lie still to try to keep the food down. I watched my brother struggle silently, and I did not taste anything I ate.

We all stayed in the living room for another hour, talking and just taking the time to be together. I eventually slipped away to dry the sheets and comforter, and I fixed up Joey's bedroom some more for when he returned. Dad and Kyle walked Joey to his room, and we all praised him for keeping down his food. My mom started washing dishes, while I cleaned up the living room. Kyle offered his help, and my dad went to bed. Kyle ended up convincing my mom to take a break, and he and I finished the dishes and the cleaning ourselves

When we were done, Kyle turned to me and he grabbed my hand. He asked me to sit with him at the kitchen table. His quiet movements and serious face made me nervous.

He cleared his throat. "Kat, I know we haven't really been dating long. I mean, like, we've actually only been on one date. But we know each other better than anyone else knows us. I know I want to live the rest of my life with you. I love you and I know you love me. Let's get married." His eyes were bright, and he held my hands in his. "I know this might seem weird to you, but the church is reserved, and it's already being catered, and the flowers are ordered. I paid for everything already. Joey wants to see us married, and I don't know how much longer he has. Kat, do you want to get married? Be honest with me."

I could hardly see him through the tears swimming in my

eyes. "Yes. Yes, Kyle, of course. Yes." His face broke out into a smile. "Wait. On one condition. This week, one evening when you are not working, you have to come to Sarasota and take me somewhere special and ask me to marry you in a romantic way."

Kyle cracked up laughing and promised me he would do just that. He said he would confirm all of the wedding details and that all I needed was to pick out a dress. We needed to get rings, and we had to figure out the details of where we would live, but those were decisions that could be made later. Right now, I was content just to be with him, my oldest friend.

Kyle leaned over the table and kissed me. His lips made my entire body tingle. I pulled back from him and giggled, lost in my delight. "You don't think Janet will do something crazy and crash our wedding, do you? Would she come and try to claim you?" Kyle assured me she was not crazy. Desperate, but not crazy.

We kissed each other goodnight. He left the house, and I went to bed an engaged woman.

19

Two weeks later, I was sitting in a tall wooden chair with a lady painting my lips red and a man coiling my hair up. The both of them fussed at me as I looked around, hoping to catch a glimpse of Oprah or Kyle.

Dr. Oz's people had asked Sandy if we knew of any doctor or pharmacist who would appear on the show with me when Oprah revealed her results from the three month trial of Venergy. Sandy immediately offered up Kyle, and the two of us had flown to California together the night before.

He had been able to tell I was nervous about what Oprah was going to say. Kyle, who did not care one way or another about celebrities, seemed oddly excited himself about the show and Oprah's reveal. He hadn't seemed worried at all, even though my career would take a huge hit if this didn't go well.

Early this morning, a car picked us up from our hotel and drove us to Dr. Oz's studio, where we were swept down separate halls, and I had not seen him since.

"Five minutes," called a man with a headpiece and a handful of large white cards.

I was pushed out of my chair and ushered to the edge of the stage. I could see the crowd and see Dr. Oz standing before them. He introduced me, and I smoothed over my Gucci suit before I walked out to him. The crowd cheered, and the APPLAUSE sign lit up bright. Dr. Oz directed me to a barstool chair at the back of the stage.

"Well, Ms. Bishop, are you nervous about the results of Oprah's Venergy test?" Before I could respond, he continued. "For the benefit of viewers who did not watch the last time you were on, we're going to play a small clip from Ms. Bishop's previous visit."

The room grew dim, and the large screen behind me showed my declaration from before: if Oprah endorsed Venergy, MedVasive would provide free samples to anyone who signed up through the website, and if she did not endorse it, MedVasive would completely shut down the product. When the video ended and the lights went up, I noticed the cameras were zoomed in on my face. I sat up straighter in my chair and tried to look calmer than I felt.

"I stand by that declaration, Dr. Oz," I stated as I bit the inside of my cheek. The crowd cheered, and my host smirked. Then he introduced his second guest.

"Along with Ms. Bishop, we invited Mr. Kyle Buffington, a pharmacist, to discuss his clients' reactions, his opinion of the vitamin, and whether he uses it himself."

Kyle walked out from behind the curtain, and the crowd applauded as directed. Dr. Oz shook his hand and directed him to the empty chair next to mine. Kyle shot me a glance, his smile bright and effortless. This irritated me slightly—*he* wasn't here to determine whether his job was at risk.

Dr. Oz asked Kyle if he carried Venergy at his pharmacy, to which he responded that I supplied him four to five boxes of the vitamin every weekend. Sometimes his customers would wait in line for nearly an hour prior to opening every Monday for their chance to purchase it. The store soon had to limit the number of boxes per customer. Kyle offered that customers who were using it looked healthier, fitter, and more energetic than when they had initially made the purchase. He volunteered that he also took the vitamin, and he had lost fat and gained muscle in the last six weeks. Kyle kept looking to me, an unusual grin on his face, as he spoke.

Dr. Oz supported Kyle's assessment of the success of the vitamin. He had conducted his own research and even had a member of his staff participate in a trial of Venergy. On the screen behind me lit up a picture of a chubby woman in a sports bra and shorts. After the audience had a few moments to review the photograph, the staff member herself came out onto the stage, dressed in a different sports bra and shorts. The roll of fat that hung out over the seam of her shorts in the photo was gone, and I could see the muscle definition of her body as she strutted across the stage.

The audience cheered as she showed off her new body, and Dr. Oz smiled. After a few passes back and forth in front of us, she exited back behind the stage, and the photograph on the screen changed to one of the face of Oprah Winfrey.

My heart dropped to my stomach. Dr. Oz announced Oprah's entry after the commercial break, and then several staff members ran onto the stage to rearrange it and brush up our makeup.

Kyle and I were moved to a small couch in the back corner. Dr. Oz sat in a wooden chair next to a matching empty chair where Oprah would sit. There was a table between them on which sat a bottle of water, a packet of Venergy, and two cups of coffee. The backdrop was even changed to a beautiful gold, silk fabric. The APPLAUSE sign lit as the show returned.

"And now, the anticipation is over," announced Dr. Oz. "Please welcome Miss Oprah Winfrey!"

The crowd stood from their seats and screamed—they did not need any prompter for their excitement. I could not keep myself in my seat. I got up from the couch and cheered with the crowd. Kyle stood with me and grabbed my hand, giving it a supportive squeeze. Oprah walked in and sat in her designated chair. She was almost non-human. Her presence alone ignited an energy in the room. She was an icon, an historic figure, and my career was in her hands.

Dr. Oz and Oprah immediately launched into small talk about Oprah's recent activities and the new addition to her family, a rescue puppy with cotton white fur. A picture of the pup was brought up on the screen, and the crowd cooed. After sufficient discussion about the dog's sickeningly sweet personality and rascal ways, Dr. Oz turned to the issue that mattered, at least to me.

"So, let's discuss Venergy and Ms. Bishop's proposition to you, which you graciously accepted. How did it work out for you?"

Oprah agreed that my proposition had been bold, but she respected my tenacity. Dr. Oz explained to her that Kyle's customers loved the product and that his staff member swore by it. Oprah commented that she had taken before-and-after photographs of herself during the trial, which she was revealing to us on the show. Just then, a picture of Oprah in a fitted shirt and yoga pants standing outside in her yard flashed onto the screen. Her new white puppy was running in the background of the photograph. This was the "before" photo.

Dr. Oz said they were going to reveal her "after" picture, but not until they returned from another commercial break. Staff members immediately burst onto the stage and filled Oprah's glass, powdered her nose, fluffed her hair, and held a mirror so she could check her teeth. No one acknowledged our existence in the corner. The crowd began to murmur and take photographs of Oprah and Dr. Oz., who were quietly chatting with each other.

"One minute!" a woman with a headset shouted, and a SILENT sign lit up for the audience. I just watched, frozen, too nervous about what was coming next to move.

"We are back, and Oprah is ready to reveal her opinion of Venergy," Dr. Oz said into the camera. "Ms. Bishop, would you join us?"

Oh, no. No, no. This is terrible.

My breath started coming fast as I got up and walked toward Oprah, who was now standing and smiling at me. I turned back to see Kyle, who nodded in encouragement. When I crossed the stage, Oprah grabbed my hands and kissed my cheek. The moment was surreal. Was this the kiss of death for me and Venergy, or a kiss of congratulations?

"Ms. Bishop, I will not go one more day without your product," Oprah stated while squeezing my hands. "It is a miracle. I have had so much energy. I sleep so soundly at night. Venergy provided me the energy and the desire for a healthy life. I don't know how it works, but I don't care," she said with a laugh. "I endorse it two hundred percent."

The audience began to cheer, and I laughed uncontrollably, the sense of relief and excitement that washed over me almost knocking me to the ground.

Oprah threw her arm around me while we turned to the screen for her "after" photograph. She was again dressed in a fitted shirt and yoga pants that accentuated how toned she was.

"You did that for me," Oprah said. "Thank you, Ms. Bishop."

At that moment, Dr. Oz announced that everyone in the audience was getting a week's supply of Venergy, and the volume of their applause swelled until it hurt my ears.

"But there's more," Dr. Oz added. I tried not to let my surprise show. *More? God, what does he mean by that?*

Oprah still had her arm around me, and I could only stand there and wait for what was to come. The room went virtually black, and within seconds, the stage was lit up in candles. A curtain rose, and behind it was Kate Nash, whose music I loved more than almost any other's. A spotlight lit up her figure as she started to sing, and then more and more candles flickered to life as they were added to the stage. I stood watching the scene with Oprah's arm around me, rendered utterly speechless.

The spotlight suddenly began to shift. From behind Kate Nash entered a man dressed in a tuxedo, dozens of yellow roses in his hands. As the spotlight washed over the man walking toward me, I gasped. It was Kyle. I craned my head to see the couch where we had been sitting, to be sure it was empty and that this was actually Kyle. At some point during all of this, Oprah vanished from my side, but I couldn't recall when. All I saw, all I knew, was Kyle moving toward me to the beat of one of my favorite songs.

As the music carried on, Kyle handed me the roses, and then knelt on one knee. He took my left hand and kissed it. With the song and the excitement of the crowd, I could not hear his voice, but I knew what he was asking.

"Of course," I gushed, shaking in disbelief.

Kyle slid a ring onto my finger, stood, and wrapped his arms tight around me. The audience was out of their seats, yelling and clapping as Kyle hugged me close. Oprah came up to us and took my roses. Kyle asked me to dance, and I could hardly nod in reply before he was pulling me across the stage.

As Kate Nash sang and we danced, Dr. Oz announced the next segment on a new revolutionary tampon, and the show went to commercial. During the break, Oprah disappeared completely and stage hands quickly swept away the candles. A man ushered us off the stage, and Kate Nash and her band were taking leave as quickly as possible.

Once backstage, it was the same as before we had first gone on. There was no Oprah, no crowd, and no one cared much about us. I was handed my roses as I stood behind the curtain, unable to move. I started to cry. Kyle laughed and asked what was wrong, but there was nothing wrong at all. I looked down at the ring through the tears swimming in my eyes. It was beautiful, a slice of yellow diamond that fit perfectly.

I gave myself a moment to pull it together before we grabbed our things walked together to the car that would take us straight to the airport.

When we were inside the car, I turned to Kyle. "How did you do that?" I asked, still feeling breathless. "How did you put that all together? How did you get Kate Nash and…all of it… all of it? How did you do it?"

He laughed at my disbelief and curiosity. "I love you, Kat. I put all of this together to make your engagement perfect."

The driver drove us to the airport and we sat in silence. "But…what if she'd hated Venergy? What if she hadn't endorsed it? The engagement would have been terrible timing."

"Oh, I knew she'd endorse it," Kyle responded.

"Why? Because your customers like it?"

"Because Dr. Oz's show told me she was going to endorse it when we planned the public engagement." He grabbed my hand and smiled at me. He was so proud of himself, he was practically glowing.

"Wait, what?" I pulled my hand away from him. "You knew and you didn't tell me? I stressed over this for *weeks*, and you knew? This was something so vital to my career, and you kept it from me!"

Kyle was obviously taken aback by my response, and, seeing the flicker of shock on his face, I started to cry again. I turned my face away toward the window as the tears flowed down my cheeks.

Kyle petted my hair and apologized quietly. He told me that he only hadn't wanted to ruin my surprise. He said he would have told me beforehand if he knew Oprah was going to refuse endorsement to spare me a difficult public reveal, but she had loved it so much, and he had not believed it was a bad secret to keep. Still, he promised never to keep a secret from me again.

I sniffled and sighed. "Kyle, I'm not mad. I get it. But please, no matter what, can we never keep secrets from each other? Can we always tell each other everything?" I turned to him and leaned against his chest.

"Yes, Kat," he said as he continued to pet my hair. "I promise."

20

Within a few weeks, Oprah's endorsement and our engagement to be married were no longer met with great fanfare and were no longer the talk of Dade City or Sarasota. MedVasive stock rose in value insurmountably after the show, and the company could not manufacture enough Venergy for the demand. The price for the product was raised and the amount produced tripled. Kyle's pharmacy received priority in distribution under my request.

Now that Venergy was moving well enough on its own, I moved my concentrated attention to Molly. I worked on the FDA package and started researching the FDA employees in order to know whom I needed to convince of what. I also prepared press releases and internet reports on the Ecstasy elements in the vaccine. I started leaking tamer bits of information about Molly to the media, and the press was soon abuzz about MedVasive's new miracle vaccine. Parents were sending me emails and letters by the thousands every day, asking for trials and samples of Molly.

My plan was to convince the public that it wanted the vaccine—no, *needed* the vaccine. That the vaccine was vital to the salvation of our children. Then I would explain the Ecstasy element. I directed the company Board of Directors and shareholders to refuse to speak to anyone about the product. The mystery and secrecy was the key to the public's support and outcry for the preventative vaccine, regardless of costs.

In the midst of all of this, Kyle and I were planning our wedding. We chose a cake—well, my mom chose a cake. Sandy and I picked out my dress. It was sleeveless, pure white, covered in swirls of pearls. Sandy all but forced me to buy a pair of beautiful Louis Vuitton shoes, which were gorgeous but virtually pointless because the dress would cover them. We ordered lilies to line the only Baptist church in Dade City, and rose petals for the flower girl.

Kyle and I planned to go on a honeymoon, but not until after the wedding. Joey was not doing well, and we didn't want to leave him, not even for a week or two and we certainly did not want to spend our honeymoon worrying whether my brother would survive until we returned.

I went home every Friday and returned to work every Monday. During the weekends, I spent all of my free time sitting with my brother in his room, helping my mom clean, and trying to keep my family's spirits high. Watching Joey slowly transform into a sickly husk was the hardest thing I'd ever had to bear—however, the intense family time we experienced gave us countless cherished moments, which, strangely enough, we might not have experienced at all had cancer not invaded our home.

While we sat in Joey's room and watched him sleep, my mother and I talked about her life as a little girl in New York. I learned so much about her childhood, how she met my father, and what she would have done had she not married and had children so young.

Likewise, I would sit next to my dad in the living room for hours on end, both of us just enjoying the other's company. There was not much talking, but the time together made us feel closer than ever. Joey's body deteriorated while our family unit strengthened.

Despite his pain, Joey was the lighthouse of our hope. He knew he was dying, but instead of being scared or sad or angry, he was content, and, as weak as he was growing, it radiated out of him.

My brother longed for relief from the disease, for eternal peace. His attitude made our hope in God such a visceral, everyday life experience.

Dealing with the reality of my brother's mortality also had the unusual effect of accelerating the closeness between Kyle and me. He spent hours at my parents' house when I was not there, sitting with Joey and assisting my family in whatever they needed. Kyle brought my mom her favorite sandwich and my dad his choice hamburger nearly every time he visited. He picked up Joey's medications and he bought groceries for my parents that he knew they simply did not have the energy to purchase for themselves.

When I was there, he and I would sleep in Joey's room in a chair, on the floor, or at the foot of the bed. We would tell Joey old stories about the three of us and our adventures when we were younger. Sometimes I would read to Joey from his favorite apps or internet sites. We bathed him, cleaned his room, and rolled him outside in his wheelchair when possible. Two or three times I placed the guitar on Joey's stomach and he attempted to strum a tune, but most of the time, he hardly had the strength to hold up his arm.

The doctors did not expect him to live more than a month. Our wedding was in less than three weeks, and we were hoping with all we had that Joey would hold out. Whether he attended in a wheelchair or even a hospital bed, he was our most important guest, and we all wanted nothing more than for my brother to live long enough to see us marry.

We had constant company over at the house from our church, from Joey's work, and visits from old friends of the family. My mom would wake up early every day in anticipation of visitors, and she tried to keep snacks and coffee available for her quick retrieval at all times. The worse Joey got, the more people that came. No one wanted to miss his or her chance to say goodbye.

One day, one of Joey's ex-girlfriends came over. She was someone whom Joey had loved everything about, but he had never truly fallen in love with her. She had been in love with him—it had been obvious to all of us—and eventually Joey had known he had to break up with her for her sake. At the time, it seemed cruel and tragic, but now it felt like a gift from

God. God had protected her from heartbreak and loneliness she could not have foreseen.

She spent an entire afternoon with Joey. She held his hand, cried, talked to him about her love for him. I overheard her tell him that he would always be the love of her life regardless of how he ever felt about her. She spent an hour talking to my mom, but only from Joey's room. She refused to leave his side. When the sun set and the moon rose, she left. She said goodbye to Joey for the last time and kissed his forehead. Mom walked her out while Kyle and I held hands in Joey's room. Although Joey could hardly speak, a tear trickled down his face and pooled into his ear. I placed my hand on Joey's shoulder without a word. There was nothing to say.

On Monday morning, the routine was interrupted when I received a call from Sandy. I had planned to work from my parents' house on Monday and return to work on Tuesday, but the moment I answered the phone, I was met with my assistant telling me I needed to get back to the office immediately. She said there was a new demand for settlement, or the threat of a lawsuit would be filed.

"That's no problem. Just call the attorney, tell him I'm out of town until tomorrow, and I will contact him by the end of the week," I responded tightly. I couldn't deny I was annoyed that Sandy was acting so urgent over such a seemingly unimportant thing.

"Kathy, the letter alleges that Venergy caused esophageal cancer to one of the free sample recipients. It says that MedVasive knew that the vitamin caused the cancer and the company intentionally hid it from the FDA and omitted it from warning labels. They plan on filing a complaint and a motion for expedited trial next Monday if the company doesn't immediately send a check for two million."

I felt sick. My stomach twisted and I could have sworn the room spun a little around me. All I could think, as I hung up the phone, said my goodbyes, and rushed to Sarasota in a daze, was of my brother.

21

I did not tell my parents or Kyle the reason I had to leave in such a hurry. Kyle kissed me and asked if there was anything he could do, but I assured him it was just crazy work issues. Once I was on an open stretch of interstate, I went for my phone.

"Darren, call me as soon as you receive this message. I need to meet with you today. I will go wherever you are to speak to you, but there's something we have to talk about."

I made sure to contact his partner too. "David, call me as soon as you get this. It's an emergency, and I need to speak with you now."

I drove a little too fast straight to the office, frustrated that neither of them was returning my calls. I had two hours to consider the possibilities that MedVasive knew Venergy caused esophageal cancer, and if my brother had gotten the cancer from *my* product. I tried not to think about the possibility that someone I worked alongside day after day would know this information, and would willingly hide it. Would I be ultimately responsible to the company and to the public if this all turned out to be true?

My heart was beating fast and my jaw hurt from gritting my teeth by the time I arrived at MedVasive. I tried not to look too panicked as I hurried into the lobby, my hoodie rumpled and my tennis shoes squeaking on the spotless floor. I then paced in front of the elevator until its doors opened for me, ignoring anyone who looked my way. Once I reached my floor, I tramped past Judy, the receptionist, in my determination to get to my office. I yelled for Sandy, and she rushed in right behind me. I set to pacing some more, this time in front of my couch.

Sandy obviously did not know what to do. She knew the letter would have this effect on me, which was the reason she had told me to come to the office, but her sheepish face showed she was at a loss of what to do next.

"I emailed you every document and email I could find in the system that mentions the words 'esophageal cancer' or 'Venergy,'" she said, sounding oddly apologetic. "I started looking through your boxes too, and I pulled every document on Venergy. They're on your desk."

"Thank you, Sandy. It's a good start. I never found out the name of the person who created Venergy. I want that information." I looked to my assistant, but before she could respond, something struck me. "Wait a second—I think I have a plan. Who all knows about this letter?"

She shrugged. "You're the only one, as far as I know. But the attorney might have sent it to other MedVasive staff."

"Okay. We're just going to move forward as if no one else knows. Call this attorney and tell him we received his letter and that I'm actively looking into the issue. Ask him if I can visit the individual he represents on Wednesday or Thursday of this week. I am going to find the creator of Venergy and find out if they knew that a side effect of the vitamin was cancer, and if anyone in this company was told."

Sandy returned to her desk to make the call, and I started digging through the boxes and emails she had laid out for me. Hours had passed before Sandy slid into my office and placed an iced tea on my desk. She whispered that I was scheduled to fly to Baton Rouge, Louisiana to visit Tony Link, the man with cancer, on Wednesday morning.

I put my head in my hands, sighed, and nodded. "That's great. Problem is I'm having no luck finding out the creator behind all this. It can't really be this difficult. All the documents I've found had the name redacted, which, now that I think about it, was probably for a reason."

Sandy leaned over my shoulder and looked at the email I was reading on the computer screen. After a pause, she said, "You know that receptionist out front that I helped you warm up to? Judy? She's been here forever, and she knows everything about everyone and everything at this company. The lady takes in information like a sponge." I looked to my assistant, who was giving me a tentative smile. "Why don't you take her to lunch and ask her about it?"

I pulled Sandy in for a quick hug, giddily whispering

my thanks to her over and over. She simply laughed. I took a minute to pull myself together, and then I walked out to the receptionist's desk with my best smile plastered on my face.

"Judy!" I cooed. "Oh, Judy. How are you? Could I convince you to take a few minutes off? It's a gorgeous day, and I was wondering, how would you like a walk to Starbucks for a mocha latte on me?"

Judy lit up with pleasure, and before she could have a chance to change her mind, I added, "Sandy will man your desk while we run out, so no need to worry." I held out my hand, and the older woman took it, and I lead her around the desk and to the elevator. Sandy slid into Judy's chair and put on the receptionist's headpiece. The elevator door opened, and as we stepped in, I looked back and smiled at Sandy, my dearest partner in crime.

At Starbucks, while Judy sipped her hot Chai Latte, I made small talk. I asked her about her family and how she liked her job, but I got little in return. The queen of gossip understood that you never offered information about yourself lest it be used against you.

Eventually, I grew impatient, and I asked her bluntly, "Do you remember when MedVasive purchased Venergy?"

Judy knew only that the drug was an enormous success— she knew nothing about the new possibility that it caused cancer and that could possibly be a huge cover-up behind it. "I do remember that the company loved the product from the start, even though they paid the original owner an extreme amount to purchase it. MedVasive paid over *double* what it's paid for any other product to date. I guess that was some great foresight, huh?"

"Yeah," I murmured as I considered her words. "Foresight."

My guess was that MedVasive had paid the extra money for the creator's secrecy. I forced myself to stay on task and I asked Judy if she recalled the creator's name, contact information, company, or anything relevant to them.

Her eyes narrowed. "Are you even allowed to contact this guy? I've heard he's very private."

"I am considering enhancements to Venergy," I lied breezily. "Various flavors, a young adult portion, things like that."

Judy blinked. "Oh, yeah, that sounds great. The guy you'll need is Phillip Landon. He's actually this personal trainer in New Orleans. His place is called Landon's Gym or something like that." She took a long, self-satisfied sip of her latte.

Judy and I walked back to our building together, during which time she offered, without solicitation, the latest pregnancies within the office, the newest couples, and some foul information I could never repeat and wished I had never heard. When the elevator doors opened onto the 35th floor and Sandy and I made eye contact, I winked at her to let her know that I had gotten what I needed.

Sandy gave the desk back to Judy and hurried after me back to my office. I told her that I would be flying out that afternoon for New Orleans. I wanted a couple of days to find Phillip Landon and to meet with the cancer victim, who conveniently was also located in Louisiana. Sandy completed all of my travel plans as I gathered up the documents I would need to take with me.

When I was sure I was ready, I left for my house to pack

for the trip. Within two hours, I had returned to the front of the MedVasive building. Sandy, who was waiting for me at the curb, reached through my window and handed me my airline tickets and my reservations for a car rental. She had also put together a portfolio on Phillip Landon.

"Good luck," she said as I took the file from her hand.

"Thank you," I responded. "Thank you for everything."

I drove straight to the airport, where I waited around an hour and a half for my flight. While I wandered the terminal, I called my mom. She told me that Joey had been taken to the hospital earlier for IV fluids to help with hydration, and they had increased the morphine for the pain. My brother was sleeping, and she was cooking a casserole for any unexpected visitors. She offered that Kyle left right after me to get ready for work. I told her that I had to go out of town for work but to call me if there was any news on my brother. She did not ask where I was going or what I was doing. She just accepted what little information I gave her and offered her love.

I called Kyle after that, but he did not answer. I left a message saying that I had a work emergency, I was about to board a plane to Louisiana where I would spend the next two to three days, and that I hoped to speak to him before I left. He never ended up calling.

The plane landed in New Orleans at 7:30 in the evening. When I was able to check my phone, I saw I had no messages at all, not even one from Kyle. His pharmacy closed at 8:00 Florida time, so I had to admit I was bothered by his lack of response.

Once I retrieved my bags, I picked up the rental car and

drove to a sandwich shop that sold po' boys (which I soon learned were just sub sandwiches) and a heaping plate of seafood. After scarfing down what felt like enough food to fill me for a week, I drove straight to my hotel and unloaded everything into my room. Before I settled in for the night, I called Kyle again. After two rings, he picked up.

"Hey, um, did you get my message earlier today?" I asked, trying to sound nonchalant, though part of me was nervous that he would be annoyed, that I was badgering him. "I was seriously busy today at work, and I went straight to my parents' to stay with Joey because my mom told me he'd been having a really hard day. The doctors are inserting a feeding tube tomorrow. Sorry I didn't call you back. I missed you though, a lot."

The thought of my brother hooked up to a feeding tube made me feel cold. I cleared my throat and kept going. "Well, I'm in Louisiana for work, but I should be back by Thursday or earlier. I'll be sure to go straight to Dade City after my flight home."

"What are you doing in Louisiana anyway, Kat?" I flinched at how concerned he sounded. "You ran out of the house this morning like there was a big emergency, and then you are flying off out of state. Is everything okay at work?"

"Oh, yeah. It's not that big of an emergency, really. There's this upcoming deadline on a demand letter, and the only way I can respond is to investigate the claim myself, so I had to fly in to meet the people who filed it. Lawyer stuff, you know."

I could not tell him the real reason I was there. What if it turned out I was wrong? What if Venergy did not cause cancer and it was all a false alarm? I couldn't risk Kyle immediately pulling the vitamin from his stores and causing word to spread. Then there was the alternative—what would Kyle think of me if he knew I had provided a product to my brother that ended up killing him, the same product I had given to Kyle for him to sell to his loyal customers? Once I knew the facts, I would tell him. I would tell him everything.

Thankfully, Kyle accepted my explanation. He went on to talk to me about one of his favorite elderly clients who had been sent to a nursing home in Sarasota. He told me that Janet had come to the store that day and stopped to speak to him. I tried to pay attention, I tried to care, but my mind was elsewhere.

"So, I guess I'll talk to you later," I heard Kyle say, and I was jerked back into the conversation. "You're obviously thinking of other things, so I'm going to let you go. We can talk when you have your head cleared."

His tone made my heart clench. "I'm sorry, Kyle. I have a head full of legal issues, and the flight clogged my ears... I'm sorry."

Kyle sighed and said that he loved me. I told him the same, but when we hung up, there was an uneasiness in my gut that I could not shake.

22

At eight in the morning on Tuesday, I drove to an old warehouse with "Landon's Gym" spray-painted across the front of it. My car bounced through the potholes of the parking lot, and I parked next to a couple of rusted trucks. I exited my rental Jeep in my business suit, a briefcase in hand, and I knew well that I was not going to fit in at this place.

There was a front desk inside, but no one was manning it. A few beefy men who looked like they had taken their fair share of steroids were spotting each other in a corner. There was another guy with a normal build doing alternating bicep curls in the front of the gym. One old treadmill sat in the back of the gym, but it looked like it hadn't been touched in years. It was a quaint place, and it served its purpose, I supposed.

I stood just inside the front door for a minute before the

guy doing bicep curls racked his weights and walked over. He wiped his hands together and then held one out for me. I gave him a pleasant smile and his hand a tight shake.

"Phillip Landon," he said. "You sure don't look like you are coming here to work out, so how can I help you?"

"Thank you, Mr. Landon. I'm here on business. I work for MedVasive, and I have some questions about the Venergy vitamin. Do you have a moment to speak with me?"

At the mention of MedVasive, Phillip's entire demeanor closed off, and he took a step away from me. He commented that he really did not have the time or the desire to discuss anything about Venergy with me. He added he had been instructed by MedVasive never to speak of the vitamin at all.

"Mr. Landon, I *work* for MedVasive," I pressed, "so you are permitted to speak to me. That will not violate any contracts or limitations. I think you have information you're not allowed to discuss, and that is exactly what I want you to tell me." As I spoke, Phillip started walking back to the empty desk. He started shuffling papers into indiscriminate piles, avoiding eye contact with me.

"I came for information, and I'm not leaving until I get it," I said as I followed him. "Give me five minutes to tell you what is going on and what I want to know. You will not be sued or accused of breach of your contract, no matter what you say. I will make sure of that. I can even make up a written confirmation for you if that would make you feel better. Just give me a moment, please."

Phillip went still, and then he sighed. For a few seconds, I thought I wasn't going to get through to him. I thought all of my work had been in vain. Then, he nodded his head and turned, waving for me to follow. He guided me through the warehouse, the click of my heels on the concrete sounding strangely out of place amidst the blaring alternative music resounding throughout the room and the loud grunts of the men exercising.

There was a cluttered, dirty room in the back with a chair and a desk in its middle. It appeared to be Phillip's office. He flipped over a bucket and pulled out the chair, which I sat in at his gesture. He sat down on the bucket and waited.

I explained to him that I was responsible for promoting Venergy, and that we had been very successful in our efforts. He commented that he had seen me on Dr. Oz with Oprah— he made a noise in his throat as if it disgusted him. Pointedly ignoring that, I told him that, from the beginning, I had provided Venergy to my brother, who had taken it regularly and loved it. Then, suddenly, he had been diagnosed with esophageal cancer. He would likely be dead within the month. I told Phillip about the letter from his fellow Louisianan, a man who had taken Venergy and had been diagnosed with the exact same type of cancer.

I told Phillip I had never been told of any risk of cancer; there was nothing included in the warnings, nothing explained to the FDA, and I had not seen one document in MedVasive's entire file related to it. I also told him how his name was redacted from all documents I had found, and there were several pages missing from the package he had submitted to MedVasive.

"No one at the company knows that I'm meeting with

you," I warned him. "I wanted to research the situation myself. I have to know the truth."

Phillip was silent for at least two minutes after I finished speaking. I watched him while he stared at the ground. "I don't know anything about that," he said. "Sorry." He never raised his eyes to mine, and my temper flared.

"That's total crap," I shot back. "My guess is you knew about the risk, you told them, and they paid you off to keep your mouth shut." He said nothing. "Phillip, my brother is dying, and others will die too. Is it money you're worried about? I don't think you'll have to return any money when the press finds out that you were paid to keep quiet."

"Ma'am, with all due respect, I have much more to fear than losing money. I could go to jail for not telling anyone about this, and that is the best case scenario." He finally made eye contact with me. "For your information, they did more than pay me off. They threatened me. They sent men with guns to my house. I had a barrel to my forehead when I signed the paperwork. They will kill me, and you, and anyone we care about if you don't stop snooping around and just shut up about the whole thing."

I was completely taken aback. Phillip said nothing more; his eyes were cold. We sat in silence for a long time.

Eventually, I took in a deep breath. "So you knew Venergy caused cancer," I said quietly. "You told them. They forbade you from telling anyone. The company probably put aside money to pay off the cancer victims because they anticipated the drug would make so much money, they would still profit even if they had to tackle a few lawsuits. They planned to pretend they had no idea about the risk, and then they would slap a warning on the product if the information ever became public."

I looked back up at him, searching his face. "Phillip, you don't have to confirm this in writing, but could you just nod if I'm on the right track?" Phillip nodded, and he whispered that he was sorry.

I thanked him for his help as I gathered my things, and walked out of his office, through the warehouse, and across the parking lot in a daze. My mind was blank. Hardly aware of it, I slid inside my rental Jeep and drove away from the gym, away from Phillip Landon, and away from the security of my life as I knew it.

I drove around for roughly ten minutes before I decided that I needed to figure out where I was going and what I was going to do. I pulled into a Starbucks parking lot and sat in my car. The radio was on, but all I could hear were my own thoughts.

MedVasive knows Venergy causes cancer. They physically threatened the creator of the drug. They've hid the information from me, from the FDA, from the Board of Directors and shareholders, from everyone who has ever purchased it.

Darren and David…they have to be aware of this. Maybe they're even behind all of it.

But what should I do? What can I do?

I decided not to tell anyone anything. That same day, I drove from New Orleans to Baton Rouge, where I would stay the night in a hotel.

During the drive, I called Sandy. I asked her to contact the attorney of Tony Link, the cancer patient, to confirm my visit the next day. She told me to go ahead and show up at the hospital in the morning unless I heard back from her. With a curious undertone, she presumed that I found Phillip Landon. I responded that I did not want her to tell anyone at all what I was doing or where I was. I told her it was vital that she keep everything between us.

"If anyone asks, tell them I'm with my brother in Dade City." She assured me she would, though I could sense the worry in her voice.

I made a few more calls before I reached the hotel. I told my mother I was doing fine, and she gave me an update on Joey. He was the same, but he spent less and less time awake each day.

Kyle could tell something was wrong with me the moment he answered the phone. He kept asking me to talk to him about it, but I told him it was just work and that I was exhausted and I just needed some sleep.

Before we hung up, I asked him to do me a favor. I asked him to stop selling Venergy and to promise to stop taking it himself. Trying to avoid the storm of questions to come, I said I would tell him about it later.

Upon checking in at the hotel, I lay in my bed for hours, haunted by what the next day would bring.

23

I woke at five in the morning, wide awake. Because it was too early to go to the hospital, I tugged on my running shoes and stuck in my earbuds. I blared old hip hop music as I ran up and down the hotel stairs for an hour.

After cleaning up, packing, and checking out, I called Attorney Black, Tony Link's lawyer, and told him I was on my way to Baton Rouge General Hospital. The man was standing in the lobby with a briefcase in hand when I arrived.

Attorney Black was dressed every bit the professional lawyer. I was hurrying into the lobby in jeans, a long-sleeved LSU shirt I had grabbed from the hotel gift shop, and bright yellow tennis shoes. I carried nothing with me, no suitcase, no papers. He looked right past me as I walked up toward him, clearly looking for a very different image.

"Good morning Mr. Black," I said as I stuck out my hand. He blinked at me. "Kathy Bishop. I apologize for my casual dress."

Mr. Black cleared his throat and assured me it was fine, and I followed him to the elevator. Once inside, he said, "I have to admit, Ms. Bishop, that your visit is very uncharacteristic of my experience with pharmaceutical companies, and with any case, really." He stopped talking and just looked at me. I admitted that this was an unusual situation and this was not the typical manner in which MedVasive investigated or responded to a demand letter.

"So why are you here?" he asked candidly. "What makes this demand letter different?"

The elevator pinged and the doors opened up to a white hall. There was a nursing station with one lady sitting at a computer, and the place smelled strongly of medicine and Clorox. The doors to the rooms were open, and I could see people lying in beds, some sleeping, some with visitors, some watching television. We passed a few nurses chatting in the hall, and in the middle of this whole environment, I couldn't help but think of my brother.

I never answered Mr. Black's question, and he did not push me. We remained silent as we walked from the elevator to Room 413. The door to this room was mostly closed. My stomach dropped to my feet, and part of me suddenly regretted coming here at all. Mr. Black, however, knocked on the door, and we heard a soft voice respond, "Come in."

Mr. Black pushed the door open and gestured that I go first. I looked at him in a way that begged him to go before me, but he didn't budge, and I sucked in a breath before walking into the room.

I noticed a young woman curled up in a chair in the corner, a blanket wrapped tight around her. Her hair was a mess. There were black rings around her eyes, and what I could see of her face looked drawn and exhausted. She jerked to life when we entered, sitting up straight and patting her hair down. Tony Link, the victim in question, was lying in the hospital bed with a blanket pulled up to his chest, still as death under the sunlight that came in through the window. His eyes flickered to us as we walked in.

Mr. Black approached Tony and explained to him that I was the attorney and representative for MedVasive, and that I was going to speak with him. He reminded Tony to refuse any questions that he had been directed not to answer. Mr. Black then walked over to the woman, who was now standing next to the other side of the bed, and gave her a brief hug. She wore sweatpants, a long-sleeved grey shirt, and bright yellow socks.

"Ms. Bishop, this is Tony's wife," said the attorney. "You may speak to her as well if you have any questions for her."

Mrs. Link half-smiled at me and I half-smiled back. Then I looked down at Tony, who was staring at me. "You don't look like a lawyer," he whispered. This made me smile, a real smile.

"I'll take that as a compliment," I said gently. "I hope you don't mind if I'm casual."

I pulled up a chair close to Tony's bed, and I sat down and silently prayed for strength. No one said a word. I could not believe the striking likeness of the scene. This was my brother. This was my brother's hospital room. I was Mrs. Link, a close loved one to a dying man. I was going to find the truth in this mess, and I was going to do what was right, not for the company, but for the people.

Mrs. Link walked around the bed and sat next to her husband so that I was facing both of them. Mr. Black stood at the end of the bed between his clients and me, ready and waiting. I began by apologizing to Mr. and Mrs. Link for their situation. I told them that, regardless of the cause of the disease, it was an experience that no one in the world should be forced to deal with. I told them that I was not here to discuss money or settlement, and that my company was not even aware of the investigation I was undertaking.

"To be honest, I don't think there is enough money in the world that could make up for this. MedVasive could give you everything they have and it would still not be enough. Not that I am at all saying MedVasive would not, or is not, going to offer reparations. I just want you to know I understand that what you are going through is horrific."

Mrs. Link reached for her husband's limp hand. I watched, and then I asked her about Tony's health and his experience with Venergy.

Her mouth drew tight, and a few moments of quiet passed before she worked up the will to speak. "Well, Tony worked out a lot when he was younger, but during the past few years, he was too busy with work and with our marriage to stay fit the way he wanted. He put on some weight—not a lot, I didn't think, but it was more than he wanted. I thought he was perfect, but he didn't feel happy with his body. When he heard about Venergy, he told me he thought it was the perfect solution. I loved him and I wanted him to be happy, so I contacted MedVasive and I didn't stop pestering them until I had a constant supply of Venergy coming in." She laughed a little, weak and disbelieving.

"He took it regularly. He lost weight, he slept great, he was full of energy, and he was working out again, usually early in the morning. I mean, he was happier than ever. He felt like he finally had it all. He told everyone about it. He was like this walking billboard. He put up pictures on Facebook and Instagram showing how he'd changed, and he always mentioned Venergy. He loved the stuff." Mrs. Link's voice faded off. She seemed to be going back to a time before her life had fallen apart. Then, she dropped her head, and her face looked crushed by overwhelming sadness.

I waited. I did not push her. Mr. Black placed his hand on her back.

Finally, Mrs. Link continued. "Then he passed out at home one day, completely out of nowhere. He passed out. I got a call from the hospital while I was at work. I thought it was strange, but I thought maybe he'd worked out too hard that morning, or he forgot to eat or something. I got to the hospital, and I learned that Tony was in triage.

"Then I saw him." Her voice cracked. "When I saw him, I knew, I knew it was serious. His face..." She shook her head. "His face wasn't right, and he was lying there with his eyes half open, like he was dead. There were so many nurses poking and prodding him, and they spent hours running all these blood tests, and taking X-rays and CAT scans. Then we just waited. We spent some time together in his room, we watched

TV. He still looked bad, but I had convinced myself he had a strange flu or something, and that the worst was over."

Tony said nothing, but he did slowly lift his hand and place it on top of his wife's. Mrs. Link seemed to gain energy under her husband's touch, and her tone changed as she continued.

"Then these doctors came in. We were ready for them to tell us we could leave." She sighed heavily. "Instead, he told us that Tony had this really aggressive esophageal cancer. He would need surgery, and we had options of chemo and radiation, but the cancer was everywhere. They said they'd never seen anything like it before. Tony, he would have only a few months at most, and that was three weeks ago. I spend every day watching my husband die."

After a respectful silence, I asked her when she had hired an attorney and what made them think that it was Venergy that had caused this.

Mr. Black immediately told Mrs. Link not to talk about anything that was said between him and her or anyone from his office. I nodded away his assertions and agreed that anything said with counsel or someone from counsel's office was privileged.

"I just knew it was Venergy," Mrs. Link said. "I know that's not proof, but I just knew. I started researching the drug when this all started. I read so much, I bet I know more about it than you do. I found information all the way back from when it was called 'Vitamin X' and it was being sold out of some ratty old gym in New Orleans. I went to the gym and asked the owner about it, and he refused to speak to me. He warned me not to visit him again. The whole thing was weird, and I knew that MedVasive was hiding something. God, I hate them. Part of me just wants to blow up their building, or *something*."

Mrs. Link was shaking now, and Mr. Black told her not to say such things. "She's speaking out of anger," he said to me, but I understood perfectly.

"Mrs. Link, you have every right to be angry. Believe me, I am so very sorry. I was in charge of Venergy since I started with the company. I was promoting it. I obtained the FDA approval and Oprah's endorsement. I provided it to all of my loved ones. I want you to know that I was unaware of any risk of cancer, but that I am currently researching the risk and I am also investigating whether anyone at MedVasive would have known about it. I'm going to do all that I can to find the truth here. I will recommend to the company to settle with you for as much money as I can obtain, regardless of what I find. I cannot promise any particular amount right now, but know that I'm going to fight for enough money to permit you to live comfortably for the rest of your life, and for Tony to be able to go peacefully, knowing that you are taken care of.

"I would give you my cell number, but you are represented by counsel, so you cannot speak to me individually. But I will give your counsel my number, and I want to be updated on your husband's status on a regular basis." I leaned forward, making sure I would catch Mrs. Link's gaze. "You will hear from me, okay? I am sorry. Sorry is not enough, but that is all I can say to you."

Mrs. Link started crying. I stood up and asked her counsel if I could hug her, and when he stepped aside, I rushed forward and took Mrs. Link in my arms. She cried so hard that her body shook, and when tears welled in my own eyes, I turned my face away. After a few moments, we broke apart, the both of us taking time to steady ourselves. I cleared my throat, looked at everyone in the room, and told them I would be in touch.

I patted Mr. Link's hand and gave him a small smile, and then I said to Mr. Black that I would call him within the week. With that, I turned and walked out of the hospital room. I went for the stairs as fast as I could without sprinting through the hall, and I took them all the way down to the lobby. I paced as fast as I could to my car, and when I was finally inside, the doors locked and my forehead pressed against the steering wheel, I cried for a long time.

This was really happening. That poor man inside Room 413, he had the same thing as my brother. Venergy had killed two wonderful men and ruined the lives of their families, and someone at MedVasive knew. They knew about the cancer risk, and they had hidden hid it, and they had threatened the only person who knew of the risk: its creator. I had to figure out what I was going to do, and I had to do it fast.

When I gathered myself together, I drove from Baton Rouge to the airport in New Orleans. I texted Kyle prior to boarding my plane to let him know I was headed back to Florida and that I would call him when I landed. He responded with a simple *OK*. That was all.

24

I did not call Kyle when I landed back in Florida. I called him after I drove home and unpacked, after I took a shower and crawled into bed. He answered on the first ring.

I asked how his work was doing and about his past few days. He told me he pulled all quantities of Venergy from his store, and that he was already receiving a load of complaints. It had only been a few hours since he had made the move.

With a grimace, I apologized as best I could. He asked me the reason I made him pull Venergy and whether it had anything to do with my trip.

"Uh, I don't know yet," I said as I rubbed my tired eyes. "I'm just doing additional research on the vitamin, and I don't want you to take or sell it until I finish."

Kyle pushed for more, but I pleaded with him to leave it alone. I couldn't talk about it, not now. I still didn't know what I was going to do next, and it made me feel cold, scared and lost. Kyle was polite enough not to press me. Instead, he gave me an update on my brother. "He's declining fast, Kat. I would try to work from your parents' house as much as possible. I don't think he has much time left. I don't think he's going to make it to our wedding…"

I started crying, and I prayed that he couldn't tell just how choked up I was. "Kyle, I love you. I will try to be home by tomorrow or Friday, but I have a few things I have to finish here."

Kyle told me he loved me and offered to come visit if I needed him. I thanked him for his thoughtfulness, hung up, and sobbed into my pillow until there was nothing left in me.

My brother would not make it to my wedding. My brother would die before his sister could marry his best friend, and it was my fault. I gave him the chemical that was killing him. It was my fault. I was the reason Tony Link was dying and why his wife would soon be a widow. I was the reason many others would likely die the same horrible death. My heart ached. I could hardly breathe. I screamed and cried and shook until I thought I would fall apart.

After I calmed down and stopped crying, I lay in silence. Five minutes could have passed, or five hours. I would meet with the Double Ds tomorrow. I would tell them what I knew, and then I would go to the press. I was certain that David and Darren would fire me and that MedVasive stock would drop significantly in value. I would lose my job, but at least I would still have my life. I just wanted to make right what I had been a vital part in making so wrong.

The next morning, I marched into my office and told Sandy to set up an immediate meeting with the Double Ds. "I will not wait more than two hours to meet with the two of them. Tell them that."

She immediately grabbed her phone and started typing away at her computer. When I entered my office, there were notes, files, and documents scattered everywhere. There was a box full of papers on my chair, and my voicemail was blinking red. With a steadying breath, I moved the box, sat down at my computer, and began sifting through the mess on my desk.

Minutes later, Sandy stood in my doorway and announced that I had a meeting in my office with David and Darren in an hour. She added that the FDA had called while I was gone. They seemed to be leaning toward approving Molly as a vaccine. There had been multiple publications on Molly in the past few weeks, and all of them included the information on the Ecstasy element, but people still seemed to be backing it.

"You were right," Sandy said with a toothy grin. "You are a genius."

I looked up at her and gave her a pitiful attempt at a smile. "I hope that drug saves the lives of millions of babies," I replied. I inhaled deeply and returned to the documents on my desk.

Sandy stayed in the doorway, and she remarked that she thought I would be much more enthusiastic about the news.

I tried not to snap at her, but my frustration still came through. "Sandy, I'm exhausted. I have a lot of work to do, and I want to finish it so I can go see my brother. You're the best, really, but all I want right now is an empty room and a Starbucks."

Sandy promised me a tea as fast as she could get it, and then, of all things, she told me that she was proud of me.

I grimaced at her. "What? Why?"

"You're doing what you think is right." Sandy looked me dead in the eye, and somehow I knew that she knew everything. She knew I would likely not have a job tomorrow. I smiled at her again, and this time it was a little more genuine.

Half of the files and documents on my desk were related to Molly. I reviewed reports from our marketing team, letters from the FDA, and research from our research team. Molly was the real deal, and it was going to save so many lives. If I did not lose my job, I was going to put all of my energy into making sure the drug got its chance. *Maybe this will make up for the lives that will be lost because of Venergy.*

I put all of the Molly documents and files in one pile, and I printed every unread email that mentioned Molly and added them to it. I planned to put it all in a box and take it with me to my parents' house.

Sandy brought my iced tea, and she helped me put my box together. According to her, I had a new litigation file waiting for me. Someone had filed a suit against the company while I was in Louisiana for a rash that was allegedly caused by one of the MedVasive brand bandages. The plaintiff was a diabetic, so the rash had turned into a sore, then into gangrene. In the end, he lost his leg.

I asked Sandy to make a file for the complaint so that

I could form a timely response. She was walking out to get started on that when the Double Ds slipped past her and came into my office.

My heart dropped to my stomach, and I sat frozen in my seat. Sandy's smile was strained as she closed my door, sealing me in my office with my fate. Darren and David were smiling and chattering about Molly; David even started digging through my Molly box. They clearly did not notice how tense and quiet I was.

Gathering my courage, I stood and asked the men to have a seat. They both sat in the chairs on the other side of my desk.

"Listen," I said, "what I'm about to say is going to be difficult for you to hear. This is going to hit the company hard, and we are going to have a lot of mess to clean up, but I think MedVasive is a strong company with a lot of great products. We will be fine, and Molly is going to bring us out of the hole we are about to fall into."

Their relaxed demeanor began to visibly sour, and they looked at each other, then at me, with furrowed brows.

"I have been researching Venergy, and in my further investigations, I discovered that the vitamin causes a very aggressive and serious terminal cancer." The Double Ds looked at each other, and David started to fidget in his chair. "I know it's shocking. It shocked me too. But it's true. We must immediately pull all Venergy from the shelves, provide a press release, and notify the FDA. I plan to schedule another appearance with the Dr. Oz show for damage control of the company. I think it is best for all of us if we face the issue head-on and we address it proactively."

David cut me off there and said we were not going to do any press release, we were not going to notify the FDA, or anyone else, and we were most definitely not going to take Venergy off the shelves. Darren laughed and commented that such a recommendation was an absurdity. He added, "You are forbidden from discussing the cancer issue with anyone."

"There is a demand letter from Louisiana," I retorted "A man is dying of this particular cancer and he says it is because of Venergy. This is all going to come out, and MedVasive will look worse if it is reactive to the issue rather than proactive."

David cast his gaze to the ceiling as if I were a petulant child. "Kathy, we will pay the man and his lawyer enough money that they will keep their mouths shut for the rest of their lives."

I bit back my comment that such a claim wouldn't matter much for the cancer victim. "I want MedVasive to pay them two million dollars," I said with as much finality as I could muster. Darren assented to that amount, as long as the attorney and everyone involved signed a release that stated very clearly that Venergy had not caused any damage, and that all involved would never speak about Venergy again.

"What?" I asked. I couldn't believe they would throw two million dollars at one case without a second thought, and I was dumbfounded at the lengths they were willing to go to hide any hint of problems with their product.

"We set aside thirty million for cancer victims when we started producing Venergy," David said.

For a moment, I simply stared at them. "So you knew? You knew about the cancer?"

"Don't be naïve, Kathy," David snapped. "Of course we knew. We know a lot of things. We have already profited fifteen billion dollars from Venergy, and we will continue to profit off of it. The few people who connect the vitamin to the cancer will be bought off."

"Well, unfortunately, David, I don't agree." I forced myself to look them both in the eye. "I am going to tell the press. I am going to pay two million to the man in Baton Rouge. I am going to pay my parents two million for my brother's death from *your* drug, and then I will quit." I stomped to the door of my office and held it open for the two men to leave.

Darren stood walked over to the door and slammed it shut. He put his face an inch from mine and demanded that I sit back down. With a stiff jaw, I sat, and I watched Darren motion for his partner to join him across the room. They bent their heads close together and spoke in hushed tones, and I couldn't understand a word. Finally, after what felt like hours, the Double Ds turned to me, and they were smiling.

David began by saying that if I disclosed that Venergy had the risk of causing cancer, the FDA and the public would never accept Molly. He explained that they were willing to have the company pull Venergy from the shelves and get rid of the product entirely. The company would explain that there was a possible contamination in one of the production plants. No one else would take the vitamin.

But going to the press would not save anyone who had already developed cancer from Venergy. Lives could only be saved by taking the drug off the market, and they were willing to agree to that. But if I exposed them, exposed the company,

Molly would never be released to the public.

I sat in silence, marinating over what my partners had said and the position they now had me him. Playing along with them would be the only way for Molly to move forward. I knew for a fact there were no secrets with Molly—I was the person in regular, personal contact with the creator of the product. I could trust this drug.

After a few moments, I asked, "You promise to pull Venergy from the shelves and never sell it again?" They both affirmed this. "And you promise to pay the man in Baton Rouge two million dollars?" Again, they affirmed. "And you will compensate my parents for the loss of my brother?" They nodded.

"But you cannot tell anyone. No one. Not even your family." Darren shoved his pointed finger at me. "*Especially* not your family."

David added that I would not lose my job that day. I was to promote Molly, get it approved by the FDA, and make magic with it like I had done with Venergy.

"OK. OK. What you guys said makes sense. I can't ask for more than getting rid of Venergy. I will pay off anyone who develops cancer if they connect it to Venergy. That is the best I could do for them anyway. I can't take the cancer away. Yes. I agree to this plan. It feels wrong in my gut but I think you guys are doing the right thing."

They stood to leave, but before they made it to the door, David asked if anyone else knew about the situation. "Just the man and his wife in Baton Rouge, his attorney, and Sandy knows about the allegations made, but nothing else."

With that, they left my office.

After some quiet, Sandy came through the door in a flurry.

"I still have my job," I reassured her. "We're going to pay the demand to the victim in Baton Rouge. Then we focus on Molly."

"But if Venergy causes cancer…" She did not finish her sentence.

"Venergy is being pulled from the shelves immediately due to a contamination at a production plant, and it will not be reproduced."

Sandy's mouth twisted, but she nodded in understanding, and she quietly stepped out of the office.

I spent the remainder of the day coordinating the settlement with Tony Link's attorney and preparing the release documents. I also drafted a response to the new lawsuit about the bandage and gave it to Sandy to be filed.

I notified her that I would be leaving for Dade City in the morning, then I grabbed the Molly box and my bag, and I went home. I planned to work the remainder of the week in Dade City with my family. Because I was still incensed, I sent an email to the Double Ds demanding that they take on the tasks of pulling Venergy from the shelves and addressing that issue, while I worked on the Molly vaccine. I received an immediate response that they would handle it, and I headed home to pack for the next morning.

25

When I arrived home from work, there was a truck in my driveway. It was Kyle. He was sitting on my porch step in front of my red door, and just the sight of him made a comforting warmth flood through me. I turned off my car, shoved open the door, and ran to him. He stood and opened his arms, and I threw myself into them.

Kyle hugged me tight and pulled me off of my feet. "Something is bothering you," he murmured. "You need me, so here I am."

I buried my face in his neck and thanked him. After standing in each other's embrace for what felt like hours, I led him into my home. I asked we not talk about work and not talk about my brother. I just wanted to escape reality for one evening.

Kyle took me to a restaurant on the beach. We sat outside on a pier overlooking the Gulf, and the sun sat low to the water. The salty breeze lulled me, and I closed my eyes and simply took in my surroundings and Kyle's presence. We shared a bottle of wine and a light, delicious meal. Throughout dinner, we laughed and talked about everything and nothing.

We finished our meals while a man with a guitar set up on the dock to play. People were starting to gather around the bar. Our waiter removed our plates, brought Kyle a beer, and I finished off the bottle of wine. Kyle pulled his chair close to mine so we could watch the man sing and play. I rested my head on Kyle's shoulder and enjoyed the moment. Then the man began to pluck the beginning notes of Jann Arden's song "You Don't Know Me." I sat up straight in my chair at the first strum, and I stared at Kyle. He stared back, puzzled.

"This song," I breathed. "This is our song. Well, actually, it was my song about you for…a long time, but this song is about you, or *was* about you. The ending is terrible because the girl doesn't get the guy, but I mean, I never thought I would get you, so I thought this was my song about you." I was talking ninety miles a minute and sitting on the edge of my seat. "This has to be our wedding song. Can this be our wedding song?"

Kyle cracked up laughing. "Sure. Would you like to dance to it?"

I jumped out of my seat in answer, and I led him out to an open space on the pier. Kyle held up one hand for me to hold and placed his other hand behind my back. We swayed to the rhythm, and I could not help but whisper the words to Kyle as

I rested my head on his shoulder. This song…it brought back so many memories of a younger Kathy, one who wished Kyle would notice her, wished he would love her.

We danced to a few more sweet ballads, and then we returned to our table, both of us tired and a little giddy. We finished our drinks and talked about the upcoming weekend. I told him I was going to Dade City the next morning, and how long I stayed depended entirely on Joey. Kyle agreed that I needed to go home as soon as I could. He did not say anything else about it, but he didn't have to.

At midnight, Kyle and I walked back to his truck, my hand in his. He brought me home, brought me to my door, and kissed me long and sweet. It was late, and he had two hours between my house and his, but as much as I wanted it, he couldn't stay the night. We both thought it best, even if that kiss made me want to reconsider. It was only a few weeks until we were married. We could wait that long.

"I love you," I yelled as he drove off. He waved back at me.

I went inside, packed a week's worth of clothes, and went to bed. I planned to wake early the next morning—I was more than ready to be with my family.

26

When I reached my parents' house, Dad was out riding horses. Mom was reading her Bible at the kitchen table with a glass of hot tea. She did not look up when I walked through the door. She simply raised her hand in recognition, and I left her alone. After using the restroom and dropping my things in my room, I went straight to Joey.

The bedroom was dark. There was a smell of body odor, and the stale heat hit me like a wall as I walked in. My eyes adjusted to the lack of light and I saw the small, motionless hump on the bed. I sat on the edge of the mattress and drew back the thin blanket. What I saw underneath was not my brother.

It was bones with skin draped over them. It was eyes were surrounded by black and a face sunk in so deeply that I could make out the lining of teeth. It was had a thin layer of hair with growing bald spots. The strong, loving, protective boy I had grown up with was not there anymore.

I stroked my fingers through what was left of his hair. Joey used to worry about me so much when we were kids. I had been a rebel, and I would climb trees or play in the road when cars were around, and Joey would fuss at me every time. When we got older, he warned me about some of my friends who he thought were not good influences and about boys who would only make my life miserable if I dated them.

My brother had been my rock and fortress for as long as I could remember. He always seemed invincible to me. But here he was, so fragile. In my heart, he was already gone.

I continued to rub his head with one hand, and I slipped my other hand into one of Joey's. It was like interlocking my fingers with twigs from the yard. I was afraid I would break his fingers if I moved. I was deciding whether I should remove my hand when I felt a slight squeeze. I looked at Joey's face, and his eyes were half open.

"Joey. Hey, buddy." My voice was horribly weak, and I cleared my throat. "I was thinking back to when we were kids, you know. You were always there, I remember. You always looked out for me."

I felt Joey's attempt at another squeeze of my fingers. He could hear me, and he could understand me. I turned my head and looked back at the door. There was no one there.

I leaned in, and I swallowed hard. "I'm going to tell you something that is really hard for me to say. It's confidential, but you deserve to know more than anyone. I am…I'm the reason you have cancer. This is my fault." I started crying, and I rested my head on my brother's shoulder, hardly more than a bone poking through his thin t-shirt.

"Venergy caused this. I just discovered it. I visited a guy in Louisiana who took Venergy and is now dying of the same cancer as you. I told my company I would go to the press, and they agreed to take Venergy off the shelves. No one's ever going to sell it again."

I raised my head and looked at my brother, whose eyes were now closed. "But that doesn't turn back time." My voice trembled as I spoke. "That doesn't save you. It doesn't make up for the fact that you would have your whole life ahead of you right now if I hadn't thrown that *stupid* vitamin in your face."

I started to shake, and I curled up next to my brother. I cried and I cried, until I heard footsteps in the hall.

"Kathy, stop it!" came my mother's sharp voice. "You're not helping him or any of us. Just stop." I sniffled hard to stop the tears, but I refused to move. I couldn't. I heard my mom walked to a chair in the corner of the room and sit down. She just sat there.

I couldn't tell how much time had passed before my brother started moaning. It started low and got louder and louder, and I scrambled up from beside him in fear, at a loss of what to do.

Mom, however, jumped out of her chair and ran to the kitchen. I stood in the middle of the room, helpless. She returned from the kitchen with a needle and injection. She drew up Joey's shirt and stuck the needle in the port that had been inserted into his chest a week before.

"Morphine. He's in pain," she said, administering the medicine as if it was a typical thing people just did on a daily basis.

When she was finished, she tucked the blanket around Joey and left the room. She did not return. Joey continued to moan, and tears were slipping from his eyes until, finally, he stopped shifting and grew silent. I tried to rouse him by shaking his shoulder and lifting his arm, but he was completely limp. No wonder my mother was not staying in his room at every opportunity. She knew Joey was unconscious to this world.

I kissed my brother's cheek and I left as well, closing the door behind me before I joined my mom in the kitchen. She offered me tea, and we sat at the table together.

"He's gone, Kathy," she said quietly. "This is all that's left. He sleeps, and when he wakes up, he's in so much pain that we force him back to sleep. We are just waiting for his body to die and his spirit to leave him." Her face was empty, defeated. She took a sip of her tea.

"I'm sorry, Mom." I could not look her in the eye, not when I knew what I knew.

"He's not going to make it to your wedding," she added.

"I know."

We sat with each other in the quiet. I took out my phone checked texts, missed calls, and work emails. I returned some messages to Kyle, who was going to be at my parents' house with dinner for everyone within the hour. I checked a message from Sandy, who urged me to review my emails immediately and text her when I was doing so.

I skimmed over the messages that were waiting for me. Many of them related to Molly and its growing success. The

FDA representative had alerted me that they would likely approve it within the next few weeks. There was an email from Attorney Black's office that caught my eye.

Ms. Bishop,

I wanted to notify you that Mr. Link died last night. According to his doctors, it was sudden and unexpected. We thought to update you in case it affects the settlement.

I could not process the words in front of me. *Suddenly and unexpectedly?* My brother's death was not a sudden thing, and the stage of Tony's cancer was not as advanced as Joey's. *Maybe cardiac arrest from the cancer or the medications?* I wondered.

But the email was not yet finished.

There is more news. Mr. Link's wife has disappeared. No one can find her to notify her that her husband has died. It does not make any sense, considering she stayed with him at the hospital twenty-four hours a day. But she is nowhere to be found. Mr. Black should be the one notifying you of this information, I realize. I apologize for the unprofessionalism, but Mr. Black was in a car accident last night and he is currently comatose. The doctors do not think he will survive the night. I do not know how we would finalize the settlement at this point. I am sure another attorney will take over the case, but there are no clients if Mrs. Link does not reappear.

Please call or email me at your earliest convenience.

Mandy

Secretary to Mr. Black

My mouth was dry, and I couldn't stop staring at my phone. I knew that none of this was a coincidence. It couldn't be. My heart pounded through my chest. It had bothered me when Phillip Landon told me that someone from MedVasive had threatened him, but I never thought that lives were really at risk, not until now.

Phillip Landon.

I needed to contact Phillip to warn him.

I left my mom at the table and rushed outside. I called Sandy to ask her for Phillip's contact information, but she did not answer. I grumbled at my phone and silently demanded she return to her desk, wherever she was. In the meantime, I decided to rifle through old emails in case I could find what I needed there. I did.

I called the number, and it rang and rang. I left a message asking him to call me immediately. I called three more times, and each time I got the voicemail in response.

I paced back and forth on the driveway. What was happening? I wanted to throw up, and I hated feeling so panicky and powerless. Just then, a vehicle pulled up and parked in front of me. Thankfully, it was Kyle and not any visitors. I was not in any position to put on a brave face and act for someone.

When Kyle walked up to me, I rested my head on his chest and did not speak. I did not cry. I did not even breathe.

27

The next morning, I woke up in my old bedroom in my parents' home, and I immediately checked on my brother. He was sleeping, and there was no indication he was going to wake up. I retreated back to my room and started working. I reviewed the files on the current pending lawsuits and began to prepare motions and discovery responses. I called Sandy, but there was no answer.

I called the receptionist, and she said that Sandy had not shown up and did not call the office to notify anyone she was not coming to work. Hearing this made my blood run cold. I had to think, so I grabbed my keys, put on my shoes, and rushed out the door.

"Headed to Starbucks," I yelled to my parents.

As I opened my car door, I noticed a white car parked on the road near the house. There were figures of a driver and passenger in the vehicle, but I could not make them out. I stood with my door half open, frozen in place. The white car's engine started, and it rolled slowly past my parents' house. The passenger was wearing a ball cap low over his forehead, and dark black sunglasses. He stared at me as they passed.

I ducked into my car and locked it. With Mrs. Link's disappearance, Mr. Link's sudden death, and Mr. Black's suspiciously timed accident, and now this, I felt sick. I couldn't think straight. I drove to Starbucks and rushed in as soon as my car was parked. Safely inside the coffee shop, I peeked out the windows. That same white car was parked next to my car, on the driver's side.

I held my iced tea close and squeezed the keys tight in my hands. When I stepped back outside, I bolted through the parking lot to the passenger's side of my car. I threw myself inside and locked the doors just as the man with the aviator sunglasses jumped out of the car and tried to open my driver's door.

I jammed my tea in the cup holder, crawled to the driver's side, and tried to shove my keys in the ignition. The man was pulling on my door handle as my shaking hands fumbled. Finally, I got the key in the hole and turned it hard. I pitched the car into reverse, backed up with a screech, and veered out of the parking lot.

The white car followed me. I sped through red lights in the small town and drove down main roads, trying to avoid any place private. I could not lose them. They knew where I lived, where my family lived.

I drove to the police station and ran to the front door with my head ducked low, refusing to look behind me. There were two officers sitting at their desks: Randy and Mark. I had known both of them my whole life. We had gone to high school together

"Randy," I said as the two officers jumped to their feet in response to me flinging open the door and rushing into the station.

"What the...oh," said Mark. The two men chuckled and sat back down when they saw who it was. "It's just you. Kathy, you scared us."

I didn't bother joking around. "There are two guys following me. They're driving a white car. I don't know what kind, but it's square and has four doors. One of them is wearing a baseball cap and sunglasses. They watched me at my house, they tried to get into my car at Starbucks, and just now they chased me on the road." Now that I was inside, I couldn't stop glancing behind me, looking for them.

Randy immediately looked concerned. "Kathy, why would anyone try to hurt you? Would they have cause to want to hurt you?"

"Yes. Well, no. I mean—I can't really talk about it. Well, see, there's a confidentiality agreement, but now people are dying and going missing..." I stopped talking. I shouldn't have said any of that, and I didn't know what to say or do.

Randy said that if there were lives at stake, maybe I should disclose whatever "confidential" information I had that could help them do their jobs. That was when I realized something: everyone that was dead or missing knew about Venergy, about the cancer it caused. If I told these two officers, my old classmates, something could happen to them too.

"Um, you know what, forget it. Just keep a lookout for a strange white car." I glanced out the windows of the station, and there was no white car in sight. "Thanks. And, uh, sorry." With that, I ran for my car and drove straight to my parents' home. I was starting to worry about them and my brother.

On the way there, I called Darren. Surprisingly, he answered.

"Darren, what is going on? We had an agreement. I promised not to speak to anyone about the cancer. Tell the men in the white car to leave me and my family alone."

Darren denied having any knowledge of what I was talking about. He said I was being paranoid, and then he hung up on me.

I drove in infuriated silence, my head ringing. I took a few breaths to calm myself, and then something struck me, something I had yet to do. I called Phillip Landon, and this time a man answered after three rings.

"Phillip!" I yelled into the phone.

"No, this is his brother, Brad. Are you a member of the gym? I guess you heard the news. Yes, I'm going to be running the gym, at least until we can find a new owner with the same image and philosophy as my brother."

I sucked in a breath, confused. "What happened to Phillip?"

"He was found dead in the gym a few days ago. He was working out after the gym was closed. They found him between the bench and the equipment with a 285 pound bar on top of him. Apparently, he was bench-pressing and dropped the weight on his head, and it killed him. I don't know how. Maybe he tried to rack it and missed. No one knows. Sorry if you were close to him."

I offered my condolences and ended the call, feeling strangely numb. I pulled up my parents' house, where both of their cars sat in the driveway, along with Kyle's truck. The white car was nowhere to be found. Before exiting my car, I took a cursory look around the street. Nothing. Still, that didn't stop me from running to the front door and locking it the moment I was inside.

"Hey, you," said my mom from the kitchen table, where everyone was gathered. "Come sit. Eat a late breakfast with us. Kyle surprised us with bagels."

Kyle smiled at me, then he took a bite of a cinnamon raisin bagel topped with cream cheese.

I gave the table the rushed excuse that I needed to wash my hands first before having anything to eat. Then I walked around the house and checked every window and every door to ensure that each one of them was locked. After confirming we were safe in the house, I returned to the kitchen. We all ate, and I acted and as if I was not afraid of being murdered.

My father was telling a story about a snake that jumped out of a tree and landed on the back of his horse. I picked at my whole wheat bagel, laughed when everyone else laughed, acted shocked when they did. At one point, Kyle leaned over and whispered in my ear, "You okay?" I smiled and nodded without looking at him. After about half an hour of relaxing at the table, Kyle said he was going to sit with Joey. He asked me to accompany him.

As soon as we entered my brother's hot, smelly room, Kyle grabbed my arm and pulled me to him. "Kathy, please tell me what is going on with you. I want to help, I want to be there for you, but I can't do that when you keep me in the dark. I know you're sad about your brother, and I know your work is stressful, but there's something more. I know there is."

My face crumpled, and I hugged him tight. He squeezed me so close that I thought simply his embrace would be able to keep me safe and erase the fact that my brother was dying in the bed next to us. And yet, I could not tell him. I was too scared—I couldn't risk Kyle getting hurt because of me.

I told him it was the stress and sadness weighing down on me. I assured him I would seek out counseling and that I would be fine. He didn't believe me. I could see it all over his face.

"Kathy, does any of this have to do with Venergy?" he asked quietly. "You asked me to stop taking it and stop selling it to my customers. That was around the same time you started acting different."

I looked to the floor. "There was a plant contamination so the company needed to pull all of it from the shelves to prevent anyone from taking the contaminated product. That's it."

Kyle lifted my chin. He looked into my eyes for a long moment, and then he kissed my lips. We spent the next hour sitting with Joey, talking to him as he lay in the bed, unconscious.

28

Two days later, I still could not reach Sandy. I wish I knew where she lived or had contact information for her family. I tried one more time, late at night while everyone was asleep, and still no answer.

Joey had been placed on a constant drip of Morphine earlier in the day, so there was much commotion occurring in the house while I watched outside for the white car or any other suspicious activity. Every nurse that came into the house was a suspect in my mind. In my mind's eye, I couldn't stop seeing one of them administering a killing agent to my brother, or breaking out guns and shooting up my family.

My parents and Kyle all commented on my demeanor and asked me to relax. I only laughed, and the noise sounded foreign to my ears. There was no way I could be calm with all of these people I didn't know coming in and out of my home.

At some point during the commotion, I slipped out of Joey's room unnoticed and snuck into my parents' room. I locked the door behind me and went straight for my father's gun case.

I attempted to open the gun case, but it was locked, and I did not have time to find the key. No one could know what I was doing, and my absence would be noticed at any minute. I dug around in my dad's underwear drawer, his sock drawer, and I patted down under the case on every side. The key was nowhere to be found.

Desperate, I pulled and tugged and turned the knob. I jiggled it again and again until somehow it swung open. With a loud breath of relief, I reached inside and started sifting through the different weapons. For a moment, I had to wonder why my father possessed so many various guns and knives. I hadn't realized how many weapons he owned, but I was grateful for them.

I grabbed a knife. I practiced opening the casing and examined the sharp edges. It seemed very effective, but the more I thought about it, the more I knew I didn't want to have to be that close to someone to hurt them. I returned the knife to the case.

Moments later, I found a gun that fit perfectly in my hand. I pushed and prodded on the chamber, figuring out how to open it. When I did, I took as many bullets as I needed out of their drawer and loaded them into the gun. I ensured the safety was on, and then I shoved the loaded gun in my pants, against my left hip. I pulled another handful of bullets out of the drawer and stuffed them in my pocket.

I worried that the one gun would not be enough, so I grabbed another, very similar to the first, and did the same with it. With two loaded weapons on my person, I felt strangely at peace. I felt ready for the white car, if it ever returned.

Once I had closed the case and made sure I didn't leave behind any signs of tampering, I unlocked my parents' door and slowly stepped out of the room. I glanced around for anyone who may have noticed me, but there was no one in sight. I traveled to the bathroom, locked myself inside, and examined myself in the mirror.

I had to make sure the guns were not visible through my pants or my shirt. I considered tying a sweatshirt around my waist, but that would make it too hard to get to the weapons in an emergency. They left small bulges at my sides, but I figured that if I didn't bring any attention to them, there was a good chance no one else would.

I placed my hands on the sink and focused on myself, staring myself right in the eye. I was psyching myself up to do what I would have to do. I was putting bravery in and taking fear out. Then, there was a knock on the door, and I jumped and crashed into the counter.

"Kat, are you okay?" Kyle asked through the door. I placed my hand on my heart. God, if I was already this jumpy, there was no way I was going to be calm enough to take out a weapon and actually use it.

"Yeah, I'm fine," I called back. "I'll be out in a second."

When I finally worked up the courage to open the door, Kyle stood on the other side. He asked me what was going on, what was wrong. I said nothing—I couldn't.

He simply looked at me with a defeated expression on his face, and then he told me to call him when I was ready to be honest with him. He shook his head, turned, and walked out of sight. I heard the front door open and close. Kyle was gone.

That shook me out of my stillness, and I ran to the kitchen and looked out the window to ensure that Kyle was safe when he left. I watched him pull out of the driveway, and when he turned down the street and disappeared from view, there was no one following him. I could only hope that he was not being targeted, not yet.

I left the kitchen and went to my brother's room. There was only one nurse left inside, and she was just cleaning up. She left moments after I walked in.

Joey was still hooked up to the IV. He was positioned on his back and propped up on several pillows, but he was completely unconscious. He seemed to have lost more hair during all of the commotion of the day. I presumed the nurses had given Joey a sponge bath and maybe some of his hair had fallen out while he was being cleaned.

I rubbed my hand over his head, his remaining tufts of hair still a little damp. He smelled cleaner, and he was wearing different clothes than he had been when I left to get the guns. The room smelled fresh and a little like bleach, and the window was open, allowing a merciful wind to blow in and circulate the air. I sat on the bed next to my brother and the guns poked me in the stomach and the leg. I laid back and tried to change positions, but I could not get comfortable, and eventually I just stood back up and leaned against the headboard.

Joey opened his eyes. It took him a few minutes, but he started to focus on me. "Joey, hey," I whispered as I knelt down close to his face. He lifted one side of his lip in an attempt at a smile.

I shot upright. "Mom! *Dad!*" I yelled. I grabbed my phone out of my pocket and called Kyle. "Kyle, he's awake. Hurry. Come back."

I focused back on my brother and lowered my voice. "Joey, can you talk?"

Joey moved his eyes around and slowly turned his head, taking in his surroundings. I realized that he was now fully conscious for the first time in weeks. I grinned at him, unable to hide my relief, and I placed my hand on his arm. It was just bone, bone and clammy skin. "I love you, brother," I said with eyes full of tears.

My parents burst into the room then, and they both rushed the bed.

"Oh, sweetie," my mom blurted, her voice cracking as she said what could be her last words to her son. "I love you. We are so proud of you. You are such a good boy."

My father leaned over her shoulder and placed his hand on Joey's cheek. "You are the love of my heart," he whispered in a strained voice. "You always have been. The entire town of Dade City visited you these past few days, did you know that? You've made your mark in this world." His tears were falling onto my mom's shoulder as he spoke.

Joey tried to talk. He was mouthing words, and soft puffs of air were falling from his mouth. He said he loved us. He said he was sorry. After the *thank you* my brother mouthed, we could hear another person enter the room.

Kyle walked around the bed and stood across from my parents and me. He placed a hand on Joey's chest and said, "Hey." It looked like it took tremendous effort, but Joey turned his head to look at his lifelong best friend.

"Look at you, man," Kyle joked, but the smile fell from his lips, and there was no humor in his next words. "I love you, you know. You're my best friend, and I don't want to live without you. I wish I could take this from you and make you better, but I know we'll see each other again."

I pried my eyes off of Joey to look up at Kyle. He was gazing at my brother, who opened his mouth to say something, but at the same time seemed to run out of energy. Moments later, in hardly more than a soft gasp of air, he said, "Please take care of my sister."

Kyle blinked and looked up at me before he lowered his eyes back to Joey.

"I'll do my best," he offered in a soft voice. No one else heard the doubt in his words, but it was loud and clear to me. I was suddenly struck with the fear that I was losing both Kyle and my brother. But Joey just smiled, and then he turned his head to face me.

I could feel myself crumbling. "I love you, Joey," I said. "I really, really love you."

I bent down to be close to him, but the movement made the guns shove hard into my stomach, and I grunted, straightening back up. Kyle watched me, concern furrowing his brow.

I shrugged it off. "I'm fine." He looked unconvinced.

Joey was still watching me. When he had my attention again, he mouthed the word *sing*.

"You want us to sing?" I asked. He responded with a brief nod.

So I gathered my wits, and I sang. I sang any song that came to mind. It wasn't long before Mom joined me. Kyle soon grabbed Joey's guitar and sat at the end of the bed to strum along with us. He was not a good player, but he knew a few chords. Joey closed his eyes and listened to our songs, and at the end of one, I let my voice trail off as I watched my brother.

"Joey," I murmured. He didn't move. "Joey." I shook his shoulder, but he was out.

The room went silent. Kyle stopped playing, and we watched his chest gently rise and fall. We knew this was the end. We understood that this moment was God's gift to us, a last goodbye.

My father began to pray for my brother's soul. He prayed that God would make the transfer from this world to the next peaceful and calm. He prayed for all of us who were being left behind.

At the end of the prayer, Kyle came to my side and lowered his hand to my waist, right over one of the guns. I pushed back in a brief panic, and he just looked at me with frustration and uncertainty in his eyes. He moved away from me, bent down to kiss my brother's cheek, and then he left the room. I didn't watch him go. I didn't watch my parents follow him out either, both of them retiring to their room for the night. I closed Joey's window, locked it, and stayed by my brother's side. I could not let him die with no one there beside him.

I curled up in a ball at the end of Joey's bed, adjusting the guns so they wouldn't shove into my body, and I listened to him breathe.

29

As the night drove on, Joey's breaths grew shorter and shallower. I did not sleep at all.

At some point, I moved from the edge of the bed and positioned myself right next to him, monitoring every rise and fall of his chest. Then, just before 6:30 in the morning, Joey took his last gasp. There were no more. No more rasping, no more quiet wheezing, no more Joey. I watched him. I waited for the next inhale, but it never came.

Without a tear, I wrapped my arms around my brother and held him tight. I laid my head next to his on the pillow and kissed his cheek several times. I wanted these last few seconds of peace before Joey was taken away from me forever.

As if my brother's passing spirit called to my mom, she walked into the room with her cup of coffee in hand. She set her cup on the bedside table before she took my brother's face in her hands and kissed his cheek. His head flopped back onto the pillow when she let go, and my chest grew tight. I pushed out of the bed, and my mom and I both stared at the pale body between us. The spirit and life had vanished, and so had any essence that it had been my brother.

I touched my mom's arm to let her know I was leaving. I gave her time with her son's body. I went to my parents' room and peeked in—my dad was lying on his side of the bed, his back facing the door. I climbed in next to him and curled in close against his back. He reached over his body for my hand and held it in his own, and then I whispered, "He's gone, Dad."

He let out a loud sigh, and he squeezed my hand until it hurt. After a few moments, he pulled himself out of bed and left the room. When I knew I was alone, I laid flat on my back, sucked in my stomach, and peeled the weapons away from the skin of my legs and abdomen. I had the indentions of holes on both thighs and deeper indentions on my stomach. I stretched my left arm as far as it would go toward the nightstand until I could reach my parents' landline. I dialed Kyle's number.

"Hey." My voice shook. "I just wanted to tell you Joey's gone. He passed away a few minutes ago in his sleep." I hung up, took two deep breaths, and forced myself to return to my brother's room. My parents had their arms around each other and they were crying over Joey's body. I pushed myself in between them. They opened their arms and put them around my shoulders. The three of us just stood there staring at the lifeless body that used to be a brother, a son.

Then something strange occurred, and it started with

my dad. Out of nowhere, my father looked to the ceiling and sobbed, "I wish you didn't have to go."

I only cried harder as my mom pressed closer to me, her hand wrapped around my head. She could barely get her words out—her voice was so thick with tears. "You were the best son I could have ever wanted."

That was when I heard the front door of the house slam shut. We all turned to see Kyle rush into the room.

He ran straight to Joey and fell to his knees next to the bed. He grabbed Joey's limp hand and pressed his face against it. He cried, and I knew he was saying things to my brother's body, but I could not make them out.

I couldn't tell how much time passed before my parents left the room, but when they left, Kyle got to his feet, and then he practically fell against me. He wrapped his arms tight around me—the hug pressed one of the guns hard into my stomach, but I could not wince. He could not know about my weapons. I hugged Kyle as tight as I could as he cried into my shoulder

When he had managed to compose himself, we walked out of the room, his hand in mine, and discovered that the hall to the kitchen was crowded with people.

My mother was on the phone. My grandparents were there, and cousins of mine were in the kitchen taking the lids off of casseroles that had already arrived. Neighbors and friends were filling the house. People were wandering toward Joey's room. Some were crying, some were talking on the phone, and others were talking with each other in low voices. Random women would hug me or offer their condolences, but all they did was smother me. I just wanted out of that house.

I leaned close to Kyle and whispered that we had to go outside. Kyle nodded in agreement, and we pushed ourselves toward the front door. Once we made it to the front porch, I spotted my dad standing close to my car. Kyle and I made our way toward him. We stood together, and none of us said a word.

While outside, we watched the hearse pull close to the back door. The driver and passenger, both dressed in suits, exited the car and pulled a stretcher out of the back. The wheels on the stretcher stretched onto the ground and clicked into place. There was a white sheet folded atop the stretcher meant to be placed over my brother's body. The men pushed the stretcher close to the back door, and then they knocked and walked inside without bringing it with them. Dad commented that he should probably go inside and help Mom with transferring Joey's body to the morgue.

Kyle and I stayed outside and watched people who were coming and going. A few acted as if they were going to talk to us, but we stood close to each other, hunched in—we were sure to make it clear that we weren't in the mood to socialize. I simply gazed down the street, where there were about twenty cars parked. The rest were scattered about in our yard and in the driveway.

I immediately noticed a white car, and my blood turned to ice. Inside I could see, sitting beside the driver, a man with a ball cap. They were here, now.

I did not panic. I did not run. My mind went strangely quiet as I pulled away from Kyle and walked toward the white car. I sucked in my stomach and tugged out one of the guns tucked into my pants. I turned off the safety and held it out in front of me, staring down the barrel as I pointed it at the passenger. The car began to back up and weave back and forth in an attempt to get away.

I started shooting. The rear passenger window was hit and shattered into pieces, and bullets slammed into the door and ricocheted off the back of the car. I continued to shoot even when only blanks were left. Kyle was suddenly there, and he wrenched the gun out of my hand. He threw it to the ground and wrapped his arms around me tight. I struggled and shoved at him, pleading with him to let me go. I could hear my father's voice cursing and telling me to calm down.

I slipped out of Kyle's grip, sprinted into the house, grabbed my purse, and ran through to the back door. I made it to my car and floored it into the street before anyone could catch up to me. I glanced in my rearview mirror and saw my dad watching me drive away, but Kyle was gone. I hated doing this to them, to everyone, but I had to keep my family safe. I had to end this.

30

I barged into the local radio station, WBRZ. I could see an older, chubby man with a full beard sitting at a desk behind a glass window, headphones on and a microphone in front of him. I banged on the glass loud enough to capture the man's attention. He turned to me and frowned, probably because I had interrupted his show. He waved his hand in a shooing motion—in response, I shoved open the door to his studio. The man kept talking into the mic, but he was looking at me as if I were crazy. Maybe I was.

I moved forward until I was standing over the man. He puffed out his chest and made an announcement that he was going to a quick commercial break. He pushed his headphones down onto his neck and moved the mic to the side.

"Lady, I'm in the middle of a show," he said in a tight

voice. You can't just barge in here. Whatever you want, it's going to have to wait."

As he spoke, he got to his feet. He towered over me, and if I were in my right mind, I would have backed off. But I didn't. I stuck my hand in my pants without ever breaking eye contact with him, and I levelled my second gun at his forehead.

Who am I? I thought in a dizzying rush as I stood there with the muzzle of a gun jammed against a stranger's temple.

"I need to make an announcement on the air, right now," I said, trying to keep my voice from shaking. "You're going to make this happen or I will shoot you. I don't want to do it, but it wouldn't be the first time I shot at someone today."

The man immediately changed face—his hands were in the air and he practically threw his headphones at me, eyes wide. He then pushed a button that lit up red, indicating we were live on the air. I told him to move to the side, and he all but tripped out of my way. I sat in the chair and grabbed the mic, all the while keeping my gun trained on the DJ. I used one hand to put on the earphones, and I started talking. I could hear my voice reverberating back at me. Once I knew I was being heard, I shook the gun toward the door.

"Leave," I murmured sharply, "and lock the door behind you. Please."

The man did as he was told. I didn't watch to see where he went or what he was doing. It didn't matter. I placed the gun on the table and swallowed. Then I spoke.

"To everyone listening, my name is Kathy Bishop. I am the Chief Executive Officer and Chief Legal Officer of MedVasive. MedVasive sells a vitamin called Venergy. Most of you have probably heard of it. The local pharmacy used to sell it. I promoted Venergy and even convinced Oprah and Dr. Oz to promote it themselves. I gave my brother boxes of samples, and he loved it. Then, he got cancer, and now my brother is dead. Another man in Louisiana who took Venergy suffered the exact same fate. I now know for a fact that this vitamin causes cancer, and I know that it has already killed two people.

"I was told by MedVasive that the company would stop selling Venergy, but I was not permitted to tell anyone that the vitamin caused cancer. Their reasoning was that Molly, a drug that I truly believe in, would actually save millions of children from contracting leukemia. So many lives would be saved by Molly if the FDA approved it, and if people trusted it, but Molly would be released only if I did not come forward about the cancer.

"I agreed to keep quiet...but then the man in Louisiana died. At almost the same time, his wife disappeared, his attorney was in an accident that rendered him comatose, the creator of Venergy died, my assistant disappeared without explanation, and two men in a white car have been following me and threatening mine and my family's safety for almost a week.

"Venergy still hasn't been pulled from the shelves, except for the pharmacy in Dade City because *I* specifically asked it to be pulled. MedVasive plans to exterminate anyone and everyone who knows about the cancer and to keep producing it and profiting off of it. They lied to me from the beginning, and they lied to me about making things right.

"I beg all of you who are listening to tell your friends, put this information on Facebook and Twitter and anywhere else you can. Get the word out. MedVasive may have me killed anyway—I will certainly lose my job, I could be put in prison for life, but I refuse to let anyone else die from Venergy."

That was when I noticed movement in the window out of the corner of my eye. Standing outside the studio was the DJ, his arms crossed and his face an angry red. Kyle was beside him, staring at me. There was a flood of blue uniforms behind them. I was so caught up in watching Kyle watch me that I jumped when the door to the studio was kicked open—four police officers stormed in, their guns all pointed at me.

One of the officers took my arms and handcuffed my hands behind my back. He walked me out of the studio, and I stumbled past the crowd that had formed as I was led out of the building. When I was outside, I managed to catch Kyle's eye.

"Kyle..." I tried, but he turned his face away from me.

The officer pulling me along opened the back door of his car, which had its lights and sirens blaring for all to see. He made me duck inside, but he rolled down my window before he shut the door. He obviously did not consider me a flight risk. He told me to stay put before he left to join the other officers and the DJ, who were talking in a circle near the door of the station. That was when I saw Kyle making his way through the small crowd.

"Kyle! *Kyle!*" I yelled through the open window. He stopped walking and went still. After what felt like forever, he turned around. He paced toward the car, and I saw that his face was twisted with anger and pain.

"You lied to me," he retorted when he got close enough. "We promised we would never lie to each other, and you lied to me. You knew that vitamin killed your brother and you didn't tell me, or your parents, or even Joey! You were going to just let them get away with it because that's what was best for you, for your other drugs, for your career. I knew something was going on with you, but this? This is sick."

The officer came back to his car then and put a hand on Kyle's shoulder. "Sir, you can't speak to her. Please step away from the car."

"Gladly," Kyle said. He looked back at me. "It's done, Kat. The marriage, all of it. We're done."

"Kyle, no." I threw myself against the door of the car as he walked away from me. "You don't understand. You don't know the whole story. *Please.* Please give me a chance to explain. I love you, Kyle. I loved my brother!"

Kyle climbed into his truck and shut himself inside before I could say another word. The officer stepped into the driver's seat and pulled away from the WBRZ station, leaving the crowd and the commotion behind.

I rested the back of my head against the seat. I had no tears. I was not worried about going to jail. In fact, I was relieved. The secret of Venergy was off my chest. Whatever happened next did not matter then. In that cop car, with the window down and my hair getting caught in the breeze, I felt a small amount of peace.

I sat there with my eyes closed when the officer commented that the DJ was not pressing charges. "And we have not been able to locate the white car that you confronted at your parents' home. We interviewed your family, friends, and neighbors, and based on the information we have, I can't say that car will show up again."

I did not move. The officer continued. "You are going to be processed and placed in jail for the time being. You will wait there until someone offers bail or the District Attorney decides what he plans to do with charges against you. If no one bails you out, it may be several days before you are released."

Without opening my eyes, I asked, "Will I be out before my brother's funeral?"

His voice was a little kinder when he said, "I don't know, but if you are not released by then, I will see that you're allowed to attend. Just know that you will have to be escorted and monitored, and you will be handcuffed."

I did not respond to that.

We arrived at the police station. I was handed over to another cop who took my fingerprints, lined me up for a photograph, and then gave me an orange jumpsuit. "Go in that bathroom and change, please," she said. I did as I was told.

I gave my clothes and shoes to the officer, and in return, she handed me a thin mattress and told me to follow her. She led me down a hall and opened a cell that had no windows and was roughly the size of my brother's bedroom at my parents' house. As I walked in, she directed the eight other women in the room to be nice, and then the door latched shut behind me, smacking into the mattress I was dragging along.

All of the women were sitting on their own mattresses—one was on a payphone in the corner. An older lady was crying and yelling things I couldn't understand. It didn't take me long to realize how hot the room was, which explained why most of them sat around in only the orange pants and their bras.

I shuffled inside clutching my mattress close as I searched out a spot to sit. I decided on an empty place next to a pregnant woman who gave me a faint smile when I settled down next to her.

"Ignore her, she's tripping on something," she offered with a nod toward our screaming cellmate.

A woman with half her teeth missing and a tattoo of a tiger on her face crouched down on my mattress. "You don't look like you belong in here. What'd you do?" I told her I shot at a car and stuck a gun to a man's head. Her eyes grew wide. "For real?" she asked. I shrugged.

They are real criminals, I thought as I glanced around the cell. *How can I stay in here with them? What would they do to me if I fell asleep?*

I asked the woman with the tiger tattoo on her face if I was allowed to use the phone. She snorted. "Yeah, good luck with that. You don't have to pay, so there's always people hogging it and fighting."

I wasn't about to fight anyone for the phone, so I just sat there, taking in my surroundings. The woman on the phone had hair cut close to her scalp, and she was arguing with whoever was on the other line. The screaming woman was shaking her head side to side and her feet were fidgeting. There were a few other women who were lazing around, all of them staring at the wall or the ceiling.

Then I noticed a short wall that probably only just reached my knees. I pointed to it and asked the tattooed lady, "What's behind that wall?"

Everyone in the cell laughed at that. It started out soft,

then it became infectious, and they all started cackling hard. I even laughed some, a little out of fear and a little out of the absurdity of the whole situation.

"That's our bathroom," she said. "There's a toilet on the other side, but no toilet paper. You have to buy it yourself and hide it from these thieves, or they'll steal it from you."

I stopped laughing. *I can't use the restroom like that. I have to get out of here.*

The cell door opened then, and everyone stopped talking. A male officer demanded, "Sylvia, come here."

The tattooed lady stood from the mattress. "That'd be me. See you later." With that, she grabbed her shirt and walked out of the cell, leaving me alone on my mattress. For some reason, that made me feel even more uncomfortable.

The girl on the phone slammed it down and started yelling profanities. I jumped up so I could get to the phone, but before I could reach it, one of the quiet girls nudged me to the side. "Sorry, newbie. My turn."

Half an hour later, the pregnant woman commented that we would be served dinner in fifteen minutes. *No way am I eating anything in here,* I thought. *God, get me out of here.*

Then I heard, "Hey, hey, you." I looked and saw the pregnant woman looking back at me. "You want to use the phone?" she asked.

I nodded desperately, and I watched her push herself onto her knees, then her feet. She walked over to the girl on the phone and tapped her on the shoulder.

"You need to get off now," she demanded. The girl on the phone turned and faced her, and the two of them stared each other down.

The lady with the fidgeting feet started screaming, "Fight! Fight! Pregnant momma's gonna fight." I flinched and put my hands over my mouth, praying that a fight wouldn't actually break out between them.

"Put the phone down," the pregnant woman said again. The other girl refused to move. Without hesitating, the pregnant woman raised her middle finger toward the cell door. Within seconds, the door was dragged open and two officers barged into the room. They stepped over me and ran to the two girls. Each officer grabbed the arm of one of the women and walked them out of the room.

"Go use the phone," the pregnant woman said to me as she was escorted out. I watched her go, baffled as to why she would do that for a stranger, but I quickly turned and ran to the phone.

I called my parents' house. My mom answered on the second ring.

"*Mom.* Mom. Help me, please. I'm in jail. Please, come get me."

It was my dad's voice that answered. "Kathy, we're working on getting you out. We finally got Bob to call the judge and get you put through the system. They're going to let you out on your own recognizances. I'm leaving the house now to come get you, so don't worry."

"Thank you. Thank you so much. I love you guys. I'm so sorry about today."

My dad interrupted me to tell me not to worry about any of that and just to stay calm until they arrived. He started to hang up. "Wait, Dad. Did Kyle help you guys get me out of here?"

He was silent for a moment before he simply said, "No."

"Ok. Thanks. Bye."

Within fifteen minutes, the cell door opened. "Kathy Bishop, please come with us and bring your mattress." I immediately stood and rushed out of the cell. I expected to see my parents, but there were just officers gathered around and one person being processed into the jail system.

One officer told me that I could change into my regular clothes. Afterward, she asked me to sign some papers and she told me that I was not currently allowed to leave the state. Then she advised me to call the District Attorney's office as soon as I had a chance.

There was an exit sign over a pair of double doors, through which I could see my parents standing outside the station. With the officer's permission to leave, I pushed open the doors and escaped into the sunlight.

31

We arrived at the house very late. Everyone who had been there that morning was gone. My brother was gone. His room had been stripped of all of the bedding and medical equipment. I took a long, hot shower that night and tried to wash jail off of me.

The next morning, I came into the kitchen and found my parents at the kitchen table, reading the paper and looking for Joey's obituary. There was a Starbucks iced tea on the table.

"Is that tea for me?" I asked.

My dad poked his head over the newspaper and smiled. "Yes, my criminal daughter." I tried to smile back, but it hurt too much.

I sat down next to them and held my iced tea close. I took a shaky breath. "The vitamin I gave Joey killed him," I said quietly, staring at the table. I could feel them both looking at me. "He died because of me. I will never forgive myself, and I don't expect you to ever forgive me."

My mom sighed. She leaned close to me, put her hand on my head, and told me that my message from WBRZ had been played on every news station, national and local, since I made the announcement at the radio station. "None of this was your fault, sweetheart. You didn't know. You were afraid, so you didn't tell anyone. Please, don't blame yourself."

"But he's dead, Mom. He's dead." I started to cry.

My dad squeezed my hand. "He is dead, but you cannot live your life blaming yourself for that. The guilt and blame is not of God, but of the devil."

"But I didn't tell either of you, or Kyle. Aren't you mad at me for that?" I looked them both in the eye, searching for blame.

They both assured me that they were absolutely not mad at me for not telling them. It would not have changed Joey's condition regardless.

"I did tell Joey," I offered. "He was sleeping, but I told him everything. I hope he knows that I love him and that I would have never given him anything that I thought would make him sick." I lowered my head again, this time thumping it on the table.

My mom said that everyone knew how much Joey and I loved each other. "No one in the world would even consider that you would purposely do something to hurt him. Now, sweetheart, the funeral is this afternoon. We need you to go get ready and forget about everything else. We just need to all get through today."

32

I drank my tea and washed my face. I stared at myself in the bathroom mirror for a long, long time. I went to my room for clothes and noticed my purse on my desk. I took out my phone and groaned audibly at the dozens of texts and the ninety missed calls I was met with. I did not even consider checking my email.

I imagined it was all bad news. I would have checked every message and missed call if I thought there was the smallest chance one would be from Kyle, but I knew he was done, and that was it.

For my brother's funeral, I decided on a black dress, black Prada heels, and I pulled my hair back in a low ponytail. I met my mom in the kitchen, where she sat with a stack of framed pictures of my brother. I hugged her shoulders and told her that I loved her. My dad was standing in an old black suit with a cup of coffee in his hand, just staring at the floor.

"I'm going to stop by Starbucks," I offered. Neither of them moved or made a sound. "Okay, so I will meet you guys at the church. I love you both."

After buying myself a tea, I drove straight to the church, even though I was early. I never expected what I found there in parking lot. There was a sea of reporters and cameras that I was forced to drive through on my way to find a place to park. As I exited my car, every one of them ran toward me. Microphones were thrust in my face and several reporters asked questions all at the same time.

"Listen," I said when I was finally given a moment to speak, "today is my brother's funeral. It is a hard day for my family and for me, as you can imagine. What I said yesterday was the truth. It was recorded and I am sure you all have a copy. I will provide more information in an official news conference some other day, but today, I just want to be with my family."

I was glad I had arrived early so my parents did not have to deal with the circus of media. Most of them dispersed as I walked to the church, but a few hung around me. They wanted footage of us mourning over my brother, but they dispersed when I threatened to call the police.

When I stepped into the church, I realized I was alone. The coffin was at the front of the vast room, sitting open on top of its base. As I approached it, I took a deep breath, my hands clenching and unclenching at my sides. I stepped up to the coffin and steeled myself for the sight of my brother.

Joey was dressed in a blue suit, his arms crossed. His face

was pale and still, smoothed out by the makeup that had been applied to make him look less sickly. He looked peaceful, all traces of pain gone from his face, and if I wanted, I could have pretended he was asleep.

I rubbed his chest. "I'm going to be so lost without you," I whispered as I wrapped my fingers around his hand. Tears dripped down my cheeks and fell onto Joey's tie. I stayed that way until I was interrupted by the noise of others entering the auditorium.

I turned up to see that my parents had arrived. I swiped away my tears and went to them, offering to help arrange the pictures of my brother around the church. My mom did not go to the coffin—she was too busy preparing.

My dad, however, just stood next to the body of my brother. He seemed to be unaware of anything going on around him. While I was placing an arrangement of flowers near the head of the coffin, I noticed tears leaving streaks down my dad's face. I thought of hugging him, but went to my mom instead and whispered to her that she needed to go be with him. She looked up from organizing her photographs and put down everything in her hands. She walked to her husband and wrapped her arms around him—I could hear her saying things to him, but I didn't get close enough to hear, just left them alone together.

I finished setting up the pictures and flowers just in time for the guests to start arriving. By 8:30, the church was so full that it was hard to move around. People were saying to me that they were sorry for my loss, and some would fill me in on their families or their flourishing careers. Standing with my parents next the coffin, I smiled as I listened to hours of stories and worthless condolences. I thought to myself how ridiculous funerals were. I understood that people needed their chance to say goodbye, that it wasn't just for the family, but I was annoyed and uncomfortable nonetheless.

After a young man I did not know told me that it was a shame Venergy killed my brother, I excused myself from the podium and squeezed through the crowd toward the front of the church, desperate for the bathroom in the front hall where I could hide and catch my breath.

I was mere feet from the door when Kyle opened it and stepped inside. We both just stopped and looked at each other. I did not say a word. Then, from behind him, Janet came to me and hugged me close and said she was so sorry about Joey.

"It's a shame Kyle's best friend is going to miss our wedding," she sighed. Then she showed me her original engagement ring. "We still have it scheduled for a week and a half from today, so we're just going to keep it and get married. Poor Kyle said he needed to deal with some personal issues and get some things out of his system beforehand, but here we are, getting married in less than two weeks!"

I congratulated her and then excused myself for the bathroom, rushing past Kyle, who was still frozen in place. I locked myself in the handicap stall and puked into the toilet. After I finished, I sank to the tiled floor and curled up there in my expensive black dress.

"I can't do this anymore," I whispered, my voice shaking. "I can't do this. Please, God, I can't take any more than this."

I stayed on the floor for what must have been half an

hour before I picked myself up, cleaned my face at the sink, and walked on trembling legs back to the auditorium. The remainder of the funeral was a blur. I was there in body, but my mind was numb. At the burial, I threw a rose on the grave of my brother, and I walked to my car alone.

I went to my parents' house directly from the churchyard. I packed all of my clothes and work documents. The house was filled with desserts, pies, casseroles. People were everywhere. I pushed through the kitchen, heaving all of my belongings along with me—I wanted to make it only one trip. I packed my car and then ran back into the house to kiss my mom and dad goodbye. I told them I would call them later.

I remembered nothing about the drive to Sarasota. I pulled into my driveway, left everything in my car, and trudged inside. There I was, standing in an empty house. My brother was dead, I had no job, my fiancé was marrying someone else in less than two weeks, and I was to blame for all of it.

33

Around six in the morning, I woke up to banging on my front door and muffled noise outside my house. Before getting out of bed, I reached over and pulled open the curtains. From what I could see, my yard was filled with the glares of news cameras and the shapes of reporters.

Not again, I thought desperately. *Not now.*

I stumbled into my bathroom. I was wearing an old mustard yellow t-shirt and panties. My hair was in tangles and my face was an exhausted mess.

I pulled on a pair of shorts and stomped out of my room to the front door. I yelled through the door for them to leave, but no one could hear me through of all of the noise they were making. I went to my kitchen and grabbed a glass plate from one of the cabinets. I opened the door with the wide plate in front of my face.

The noise grew deafening and people started pushing themselves toward me. I had to steady my feet to keep from falling back. I held the plate with my right hand and grabbed at one of the multiple mics that reporters were attempting to shove under the plate.

"Listen, I will give a press statement," I blurted. When some of the voices quieted down, I continued. "I am going to MedVasive this week to sort out my position with the company. I am also meeting with the District Attorney in Sarasota to discuss the future of David and Darren. I plan to press charges against them on behalf of my family, my assistant, and everyone else who has been harmed by Venergy or MedVasive."

I thrust the microphone back into the crowd, and the moment I felt a hand take it from me, I backed into my home and closed the door. I locked it and spent a few minutes pacing around my house, trying to calm myself down. After a little while, I peeked through the front window and noticed most of the crowd had left, a few stragglers still waiting around in front of the yard.

I took a rushed shower, after which I called the District Attorney in Dade City, Robert McManus. I told the receptionist who I was, and she patched me right through to him.

"Kathy Bishop," he greeted me. "We have to have security here for all our reporters because of you. The whole country wants to know what we're going to do with your case. You doing okay? I know you just lost your brother."

I replied to my senior prom date, "Yeah, sorry for the inconvenience." He laughed and said he enjoyed the publicity and that it would probably be good for his reelection campaign.

I sighed. "Robert, I shot at two men who had been following me for days, probably trying to kill me. It was complete self-defense." I paused to determine if he was in agreement.

"Yes, but you stuck a gun to the head of a poor, innocent DJ." Robert responded with a chuckle. "But he is not pressing charges, right? Because he thought you were brave and he understood what you were doing. But I don't need him to press charges to bring a case against you. You know that."

"Yes, I know that." I sighed some more. "I don't want to go back to jail, Robert. The women in there will eat me alive."

He responded that the only thing he cared about was handling this situation in a way that was best for his career. "Spoken like a true politician," I said with a huff. "So, what is good for your career?"

"I'm going to enter a plea agreement with you," he answered. "The shots you fired at the white car did not injure anyone, and it was self-defense. No charges are being brought against you for that incident. In fact, we're asking anyone and everyone for information on that car because we suspect its occupants to be involved in several murders and disappearances that have occurred over the past few weeks. I am charging you, and you will plead guilty to, simple battery of the DJ. The plea agreement provides that you sentence is three hours of news reporting for WBRZ.

I narrowed my eyes in confusion. "How exactly am I going to report the news?"

"You'll talk about Venergy, how you found out it causes cancer, your relationship to the guys who knew about it, your experience at the company. You will give this report prior to speaking with any other press so that Dade City gets national recognition. I'll be on the radio station with you along with the DJ you threatened to kill. I will be mayor in four years, the DJ gets serious exposure, and you don't lose anything. All you have to do is sign the plea agreement to simple battery."

I agreed to these terms, but I made it clear that I could not be obligated to disclose anything about my personal life that I didn't want to in the report. Robert agreed, and we scheduled the plea agreement and the radio show for the day before Kyle's marriage. I had planned to go to Dade City anyway to be with my parents during the wedding weekend.

I knew that as soon as we hung up that he would be notifying all of the local newspapers, radio stations, and television stations about the upcoming exclusive first interview with Kathy Bishop.

34

After my call with Robert, I drove to the office of the Sarasota District Attorney. My yard was empty of reporters and no one seemed to be following me. I still had not turned on my phone or laptop yet. I was just not ready for work drama.

I pulled into the District Attorney's office and notified the receptionist of my meeting with him. She asked me to have a seat. Within a few moments, Attorney Sam Jones walked into the lobby and held out his hand.

"Sam Jones. Nice to meet you, Ms. Bishop."

There were a few assistant attorneys in the room he led me to, all of them sitting at a conference table with yellow legal pads, pens, highlighters, and folders full of documents scattered atop it. There were a few photographs spread around the table. All of the attorneys stood and introduced themselves as they took turns shaking my hand. Then I sat at the head of the table opposite Attorney Jones.

He began to explain the situation. "After your announcement, we confiscated all of MedVasive's records on Venergy. We sent out two teams of police to David and Darren's homes and arrested them both. They are being held in prison with no bonds available because they are a flight risk. We are now treating the disappearance of your assistant, Sally, and that of the wife of Tony Link, as murder investigations. We are also retrieving Tony Link's body from the morgue to determine his exact cause of death. We sent an investigation team to The Landon Gym to look for evidence of foul play or anything related to the other victims.

"We have not located the white car, and no one has provided any credible evidence on the identities of the two men you saw. We are charging David and Darren with first degree murder, conspiracy, and multiple other charges. I believe they will never see the outside of a jail cell again. We fully expect the Department of Justice to bring civil claims against them as well. I should also mention that their bank accounts have already been frozen, so no money will be available to either of them."

All of this information delighted me. It felt like…like justice. The Double Ds were getting what they deserved.

I smiled and asked how I could assist. My hosts told me they needed me to disclose everything I knew about Venergy, about the documentation and my investigation. I agreed to discuss with them anything they wanted to know, as long as I could sign an indemnity agreement stating that no criminal or civil claim could be brought against me.

Attorney Jones pushed a document toward me from across the table. "Done," he said.

I read the indemnity agreement over and signed it. Then I told them everything I knew. They said that I would be a witness in the trial against the Double Ds and that they would need the documents I had mentioned that had missing pages and redacted information. I promised to deliver them as soon as I could. I explained that I planned to go to MedVasive the next day to retrieve my personal belongings.

One of the attorneys asked me if MedVasive had fired me. "I presume so." I replied with a shrug. Then I couldn't help but feel a little worried for the company. "Are there going to be any civil claims brought against MedVasive?"

Attorney Jones said that he did not know, that such things were the Department of Justice's territory. He was sure, however, that the company would be audited and their documentation reviewed.

We finalized the meeting with a secretary handing me a copy of the executed indemnity agreement, a promise to bring them the documents they requested and a promise that I would cooperate in any way requested. I shook hands with all of the attorneys again, and then headed home.

I considered what I would do next, with the increasing likelihood that my position at MedVasive was no more. I had enough money to hold me over for several months. I knew I would be busy for a few weeks with the aftermath of the Venergy scandal. During that time, I planned to figure out what I wanted to do with the rest of my life.

35

The next morning, I dressed in one of my red designer suits. I chose red because if I ran into anyone from the company, I wanted to feel fearless. A black suit could give the impression of mourning, of guilt. I drove to MedVasive to gather my things, grab the documents for the District Attorney and to drop off everything I had of theirs in my possession. I hoped to get in and out before all of the employees arrived.

When I arrived, I grabbed my two boxes of documents and stacked them on top of each other. They towered over my head as I walked through the front door of the building, and I paced quickly toward the elevator, hiding my face behind the boxes.

"Ms. Bishop," I heard from a voice call from near the security table. I sighed and turned to face whoever had said my name.

"Hi," I said apologetically. "I need to drop off these boxes. Am I permitted to go to my office, or do I need an escort? I would offer for you to just take them up, but I would like to get the rest of my belongings out of my office."

The security guard who had said my name smiled broadly and said that he would be honored to escort me up. He offered to hold the boxes for me, and I smiled back at him, a little confused by his warmth and enthusiasm.

On the way up to my floor, the guard commented that he thought what I had done on the radio was brave and that he was proud of me. I looked at him in shock. "Thanks," I said quietly.

He chuckled and asked in a low voice, "Did you actually shoot up that car?" I couldn't help but snort a laugh, and I admitted that yes, I had. He shook his head. "Crazy white girl." That made me laugh louder.

When the elevator reached my floor, we turned on the lights to the reception area and walked down the long hall to my office. We dropped the boxes on the floor and I thanked the guard for his help. I closed the door behind him when he left.

I did not have many personal items at my office, so one box was sufficient to gather them all. It took ten minutes, and I was hoping to leave the building before any more people arrived. I had no desire to face them, all of the employees I had come to know during my time here. If my press release caused MedVasive to fail, then all of them would lose their jobs, and I knew whom they would blame. I opened my office door, ready to make a break for the elevator, when Sandy's desk caught my eye.

My heart sank. *Poor sweet, wonderful Sandy.* I walked slowly to her desk, almost afraid that any move I made would mess up how normal everything seemed. It looked as if she would arrive at any moment. No one had cleaned off her desk, or gathered up her belongings.

I returned to my office and grabbed another box. I then went to Sandy's desk and carefully cleaned it off of all of her personal items. I could not stop the tears from falling when I grabbed the tape holder shaped like a high heeled shoe I had purchased for her because I knew she would love it. Her reaction had been priceless—she had run around the entire floor and shoved it in everyone's faces.

Sandy had cared for me, and she too had lost her life because of me. If I had gone straight to the press after I returned from Louisiana, she would probably still be alive.

I filled her box as quickly as possible. As I was stuffing her hair products together inside, I decided that I was going to contact her family and see if they had yet done any memorial for her yet. I wanted to do something for Sandy, anything.

Before I finished up, I heard the elevator open and several people walk into the reception area. I heard Judy sit in her chair and I heard others moving down the hall. Now feeling anxious, I closed up Sandy's box tight, stacked it on top of mine, and I started toward the elevators.

I said nothing as I passed Judy, and I pushed the button for the elevator with my elbow. Judy jumped out of her seat and ran over to me. I flinched away, expecting the worst, but instead she grabbed my arm and said, "Thank you for doing what was right, Kathy. Everyone is so proud of you."

"What?" I asked in bewilderment. "You guys could lose your jobs. Aren't you mad at me?"

Judy responded that no one was mad. Just the opposite. Everyone considered me the hero of MedVasive. "The shareholders and Board of Directors have met multiple times about the future of MedVasive and how to clean up the company's reputation, and what to do with you."

"With me? What do you mean?"

"Everyone wants you to stay and to run the company. They think you standing behind the firm would be what it takes to keep MedVasive from going under."

I thanked Judy for the information as I stepped into the waiting elevator. "Really, thank you," I said more sincerely than I had ever been with her.

This was a complete turn of events for me. I had never considered that I still could work at MedVasive after all that had happened. Now that the Double Ds were out, the evil of the company had been eradicated, or so it seemed.

Do I even still want to work there? I thought as I walked to my car. *Is that what I should do, stay and help clean up the company? Should I go down with the ship or jump out now? If I saved the company, I could be heralded as some sort of miracle executive officer. Something like that could get me any job I want at companies four times as big as MedVasive.*

Once I drove home, I changed into my workout clothes and I went for a run. I wanted to clear my mind so I could decide what I wanted to do with all of the information and decisions that had been thrust upon me over the past few days.

I ran Siesta Beach with my music blaring, and I watched

waves softly crash onto the sand and people tanning in chairs. I weaved around children building sand castles and kids running from the water to their parents and back again. The longer I ran, the lighter I felt.

I ran the entire span of the beach before I turned around to run back. On the way, I was plagued by thoughts of Joey, of how hard life was going to be without him. I was angry and sad about Kyle and Janet. I felt pity for my parents, who had lost their son. Sandy was on my heart as well. The run was forcing all of those feelings to push through my pores.

What will I do if I leave MedVasive? What will my options be?

I could go back to my old law firm and ask them for a position. I have confidence they would take me back.

I could open my own firm. I could open an office in downtown Sarasota. I could advertise my new firm during upcoming press conferences and explain why my new passion is for helping those hurt by people like the Double Ds.

When I reached the end of the beach where I started, I turned around and walked some more—I had not yet made up my mind about the things swirling around in my head, and I wanted more time to think.

I wished there was a way I could save Molly. It had such potential. I could buy it from MedVasive. I could open a pharmaceutical company and produce the drug myself. Actually...I could do both.

There was no reason why I could not protect those injured by bad pharmaceutical and medical device companies and, at the same time, produce quality products and medicines. However, the more I considered it, I realized I would have to open two separate companies so there was no conflict issue.

That was my decision. I was going to do both.

I would take all of my savings to purchase Molly from MedVasive and produce that vaccine because I believed in it. I wanted to save children from leukemia. I wanted to help people in every way that I could. Maybe that could help make up for all of those who had died because of me.

I returned home and showered, feeling all at once heavy and energized by my thoughts. I called a local, well-known real estate agent and scheduled a meeting with her for the next day for two separate buildings: law firm and pharmaceutical company.

I made contact with NBC, Dr. Oz, Oprah, ABC, and Fox and set up interviews as they had previously requested to discuss all I knew about Venergy. I planned all of the interviews to take place after my required WBRZ news report.

While I had been out running, the acting officer of the Board of Directors of MedVasive called and left me a message. He said he heard that I was back in town and that I had come by the office to get my things. He wanted to speak to me about my future with MedVasive and my contract. I had forgotten about my employment contract. I needed to review it so that I could go to the meeting ready to argue any and all of my positions.

I called Bruce, the acting officer, and agreed to meet with the Board on Thursday, then I dug around in my kitchen drawers until I found my contract. I scribbled notes on the back of the document to prepare my arguments for my exit from the company, as well as the severance requirements for the upcoming Board meeting.

I spent the remainder of the day investigating startup pharmaceutical companies, physicians who have expertise in medical devices, calling my parents, and searching commercial real estate in Sarasota area.

When that was finished, I called Judy and asked her for any family contacts for Sandy. She provided to me the number for Sandy's mother, Jill, whom I immediately called. When she answered, I suddenly realized that I had no idea what to say.

"…Hi, Ms. Jill," I eventually settled with. "This is Kathy Bishop. Sandy was my receptionist. I loved her very much. I am so, so sorry for your loss."

Sandy's mother was kind. She told me that the police had located Sandy's body near Anna Maria Island two nights earlier and that she and the rest of the family were not yet permitted to see the body. I asked if I could give, or assist in giving, Sandy a memorial, and Jill said that they were putting together a memorial for that afternoon. It was going to take place on Anna Maria Island.

36

A week after my brother's funeral, I had to attend a meeting with the Board of Directors and majority shareholders of MedVasive to discuss my future at the company.

I was forced to push my way through the media and onlookers who were loitering outside of the building. Microphones were pushed in my face and voices shouted at me, asking me what I was going to do and whether I thought MedVasive's stock could ever come back from its recent crash. I smiled and said nothing.

MedVasive paid security for the inside and outside of their building, so I found myself quickly escorted inside by two large men in suits and dark sunglasses. Neither said a word to me. I walked into the elevator alone in my conservative grey dress suit with black and silver stilettos. I carried my matching leather briefcase, which held my employment contract that I had tagged and highlighted, and the articles I had printed on Venergy. I was prepared with research and news reports about the numerous lies, the hidden defects, and the risks that Darren and David had taken on multiple products over the past several years.

I took a deep breath as the door opened, and I walked out with my head held high. I was ready to quit my job at MedVasive and walk away with either a hefty severance or the rights to Molly. Either way, I was ready to be free.

Judy came around from her desk and gave me a tight hug. "Good luck," she whispered in my ear. Then she ushered me into the main conference room. I was shocked by what I saw when I walked through the door.

The enormous table was completely full—there were chairs lining the walls and people were crouching on the floor and standing in clumps around the room. There were hundreds of them, and the room suddenly felt much smaller.

As I walked in, the mumbling and noise ceased, leaving pure silence. Then, a man at the conference table stood up and started to clap. Everyone followed suit, and the entire room began clapping and cheering for me. I couldn't understand it. Their company, their money, their livelihoods, all of it had just tanked because of me.

They should be booing me and threatening to sue me.

Although confused, I was honored that the room supported me—for the moment anyway. I smiled and cocked my head to the side as a small courtesy. The acting officer of the Board of Directors stood at a podium in the corner of the room farthest from the door. He told everyone to quiet down so we could get down to business. There was nowhere for me to sit, and I did not really know where I was supposed to stand, so I just stood awkwardly inside the doorway.

The acting officer started the meeting with a roll call, ensuring there was a quorum for a decision to be made. Then he began.

"As you all know, Darren and David, who started this company and who were in charge of many of its products, concealed risks and dangers of those products and are being accused of conspiracy, assault, battery, murder, and RICO violations. They are about to be indicted, and the company is not standing behind them based on the evidence which has come forth after recent investigations.

"There may be fines and claims brought against MedVasive depending on what is found by the Department of Justice. As far as any of are concerned, there is nothing in this company that violates any rules or regulations, but none of us know just what David and Darren have done, or what all they have hidden.

"After Kathy Bishop revealed the recent cancer risk of Venergy and the press learned of the violent acts related to this company, they began to investigate. The public is aware of the multitude of devices that could also have risks and dangers, all of which were hidden from them and from the FDA. In the past few days, we have had over a hundred lawsuits filed against the company from consumers and doctors. MedVasive may owe thousands or millions of dollars in fines to the federal government in addition to the costs of the lawsuits being filed.

Not to mention our Defense Attorneys are billing us around the clock.

"Our stock is now worthless. No one is purchasing MedVasive products and doctors are refusing to use or promote anything with our name on it. We have to make a decision for moving forward. Today's discussion is going to be one that will end in a resolution. We do not leave this room until we have a plan of action. I am going to offer some recommendations to get started, then we will, in an orderly fashion, plan the future of MedVasive, and also plan Ms. Bishop's position with the company."

There was a long pause to allow everyone to prepare, and to make sure people were paying attention.

"One option," said the acting officer, "is to file bankruptcy, close the company, and cut our losses." The crowd moaned at that.

"Another option is to publicly announce that the company was a victim of David and Darren just as much as the public, and that we are paying for multiple consultants to reevaluate every product we are currently selling. We will also have an outside consultant firm that will evaluate every product prior to our submission to the public or to the FDA as a way to prevent this ever occurring in the future. We start pushing publicity of MedVasive employees and shareholders performing charity for those who have been hurt by our products. Footage of going to funerals, visiting the sick, buying homes for family members left behind because of our company. We do all we can to change the public's opinion of our company and try to convince everyone that this was solely David and Darren's doing.

"This will be costly, and we will also have the costs of the lawsuits and the possible government fines to deal with. But if we want to try to save this company, it's going to take everything we have. We will all have to be financially dedicated. If there are shareholders or director members who are not interested, we will have a buyout plan if this is the option we choose."

He then asked if anyone had any recommendations. A tall blonde woman stood up and said that the only way the company would survive is if Kathy Bishop stood behind it.

"Kathy would need to do press conferences, she would need to stand up for the company," she said. "She is the nation's hero right now, and we need her to be our spokesperson if your second option is going to work. The people want to see her going to the funerals, going to visit the sick. They want to see her promising protection. Her brother died, she was almost killed—if she still believes in this company, that would say so much to the public."

The room clearly agreed. "Yes!" they yelled.

"It's the only way."

"That has to be the plan."

The acting officer met my eye then, and I walked up to meet him at the podium. I turned to the crowd and thanked them all for their support and confidence in me. "I came here expecting to be bullied and verbally abused for my press release. I thought you would blame me for the fall of the company. I never expected this reaction." I had to laugh a little. "I came here ready to put up a fight, and now I feel completely unprepared."

The acting officer said to me that I had to decide whether I would stay with the company or leave. He said that if I stayed, either I would pull the company out of hole or I would go down with the ship. He assured me that the room was confident I could save MedVasive and that, if I did, it would be historical for the company and for the accomplishments of women in corporation as a whole.

"Show the world that a woman can uncover a man's lies and deceits and save an entire company from that man's destruction," he said.

The blonde woman who was still standing said, "Do it for us women. Do it for the employees of this company. Do it for revenge. Show the world that you do not put up with the injustice, or do you turn your back on the company. Show them that if you go down, you go down fighting."

The room fell silent and everyone stared at me. I couldn't speak, couldn't move.

I had wanted to quit. I had wanted to start my own firm to help people. I had wanted to buy Molly and start my own pharmaceutical company, and I had never wanted to hear the word "MedVasive" again. Now, I was without any idea of what to do.

Hundreds of people sat, or stood, watching me. I closed my eyes and I prayed for guidance. I prayed that I would do the right thing.

No one moved. No one said a word. After over five minutes of standing at the podium with my hands on each side of it and my head down, I started to speak.

"I came here to quit," I said, almost a whisper. My next words were louder. "I came here to demand my payout and possibly purchase Molly. I wanted nothing to do with this place. As far as I'm concerned, this company killed my brother and tried to kill me. They killed Sandy, who was loyal and hardworking, and whom I loved so much, and they killed other innocent people. I wanted to leave and start my own firm to represent others who have been hurt by pharmaceutical companies, companies like this one.

"But seeing you all today, hearing what you have to say, I feel like you genuinely want to do the right thing. This is not a shady corporation. This is a strong, thoughtful company that fell victim to two thugs. I was one of those victims, and I played along without even knowing it." I paused and waited a few moments to make sure I was ready to make a commitment before continuing.

"I will stay under several conditions. If not all of my conditions are met, I will leave. I ask that all MedVasive products, every single one, be pulled from the shelves. We can't trust that any of those products are safe. We move forward with new products only, and Molly will be pushed hard as our first new drug.

"We keep all of our staff except for ten to fifteen employees who I believe were involved with David and Darren. We pay employee salaries before our own and before dividends or bonuses.

"We all promise to personally visit every person who claims to have been injured by our products. There will be fakers, probably, but we will treat them well all the same. I will personally handle the government investigations and fines. I believe I can prove to them that MedVasive was a victim and should not be punished. Rather, the company is being punished enough with the extreme losses it has suffered this year.

"We give as much as we can afford to the victims and we show them genuine love and support. We attend all funerals of people who have died and will die from Venergy, and we notify the press when we do so.

"We permit our company one year through this struggle, and if the company stock does not go up, or if lawsuits drain us into bankruptcy, then we fold and go quietly.

"For this to really work, every single one of us needs to be hustling to find new products. We cannot make money without them. I will meet with each creator we find, personally review the research, and put my stamp of approval on all products we decide to purchase. We will also have an outside company that will review every product before we put it on the market."

The acting officer looked to me to determine if I was finished. When I stepped back from the podium, he took the stand and announced it was time for a vote. "Anyone for filing bankruptcy?"

No one spoke.

"Anyone for Ms. Bishop continuing to act as Chief Legal Officer and Chief Executive Officer for MedVasive?" The entire room began to cheer, and one by one, they stood from their seats. It was unanimous.

The room was chaos after that. People were shaking each other's hands and hugging. The acting director pulled me close and shook my hand, whispering to me his heartfelt thanks.

"Don't thank me yet," I said. "Thank me in a year, if this works."

He chuckled, then promised me he would draft up a new employment contract. We agreed that I would start the next day and he would have the contract ready before then.

I began to walk out of the conference room, and the entire crowd followed me. I exited the MedVasive building with all of them at my back, and we and stood at the top of the three steps that led down to the sidewalk. There were at least a dozen news crews there, all of them shoving microphones at my face, and hundreds more people surrounded the area.

I stood and smiled. I waited for a lull in the noise, and then I made my announcement.

"Ladies and gentlemen, thank you for being here and taking such interest in the future of this company, and in my future. Venergy killed my brother, along with many innocent people. David and Darren, the two creators of MedVasive, are responsible in killing my assistant and many others for whom I cared. As angry as I am, my anger is toward the wrongdoers, not the victims. Just as my brother did not know Venergy would kill him, neither did I know that the vitamin I was giving him would cause him cancer. None of the Board of Directors, shareholders, or employees of MedVasive knew this either. Many of us, most of us here at MedVasive, also took Venergy because of how effective it was. We were all victims.

"The only way to ensure that MedVasive does not put another dangerous product on the market is by destroying all of MedVasive's current products and devices. The company is pulling every single one of its products regardless of the cost.

There is no way to know what other products may have life-threatening risks that were hidden by David and Darren, so they all must go.

"Moving forward, I will personally scrutinize every new product we are interested in selling, and we will retain an outside company to review everything about the product. If that company does not give its approval, then the product will not be marketed. There is one new drug that we already have in the works. We're calling it Molly, and it is a product that I started. I did all of the research and investigation into it myself. Molly is going to be the first in a new line of clean and honest products.

"Finally, to all of the individuals who have been hurt in any way by MedVasive's products, I want to tell you how sorry I am. We are all sorry, truly sorry. Please, contact me with any funeral arrangements, hospital room numbers, or addresses of anyone who is suffering from a MedVasive product, and we will personally visit you and attempt to help you in any way that we can. The company will take responsibility, and we will do the right thing for all of those who suffered and continue to suffer.

"I believe in this company," I said, my voice shaking. "I believe in Molly. I believe MedVasive is a great American enterprise that can pull through this tragedy. Thank you."

I started to walk through the crowd while reporters yelled questions at me. The bodyguards at either side of me shielded me with their arms on the way to my car. I slipped into my car, shut out the noise, and drove home.

I could not believe how the day had turned out. I could

not believe I was still working for MedVasive. The only thing I needed to know now was what my parents thought about me working for the company that had killed their son.

37

I packed and drove from my house to Dade City for Kyle's wedding. I knew my parents would need me there. They loved Kyle like a son—he had been Joey's best friend, and they had been looking forward to him being the husband of their daughter. I did not plan to go to the wedding, but the least I could do was spend the weekend with my mom and dad.

When I arrived at my parents' house Friday morning, they were in their room. I crept in to find them still in bed. "I'm home," I whispered as I crawled into bed between the two of them.

My mom patted my leg and said she heard I was going to be talking on WBRZ that day. I laughed and said that I was helping the District Attorney run for mayor. My dad huffed and said something about crooked politicians.

He then commented that I was the talk of all the news channels. I had even been discussed on his hunting show. They had made a comment that I should be a guest on their show after the way I shot up the white car. "The guy said you were a real tough cookie."

I laughed with him. "Yeah, right," I said. "I don't think so."

My dad stopped laughing. He took my face in his hand and locked eyes with me. "Kathy. You are tough. You are mentally tough. You are spiritually tough. You are the strongest person I know. You are also very, very smart. Keep up the work you're doing, I mean it. We are so proud of you for staying with your company and working to make it right and honest. You are making history."

I wrapped my arms around him tight. His approval meant so much to me. "Thank you, Dad." Then I let him go and hugged my mom and told her I loved her too. I couldn't help but notice an emptiness in the room, the lack of my brother.

Mom said that she was going to start cleaning out Joey's room. She asked me to take anything of his that I wanted to have with me. Also, they were going to empty his home and sell it. They were putting it on the market in a month. I promised to spend the day helping them decide what to save, what to give away, and what to throw out, but only after my ridiculous "community service" at WBRZ.

I spent another thirty minutes with my family, then I left for the radio station. The District Attorney and the DJ were in the studio waiting for me, the latter of which I noticed seemed to avoid speaking to me, making eye contact with me, acknowledging that I existed.

When I was put on the air, we talked about MedVasive. We discussed all of the details of the white car, and I attempted to recall information about the occupants. A few callers were very supportive of me staying with the company, and other callers reamed me a new one, accusing me of "sleeping with the enemy."

One caller refused to provide his name. "Yes, mystery man," said the DJ, "what is your question?"

The caller hesitated before he asked, "Ms. Bishop, after you found out that Venergy caused cancer, did you think that anyone else who knew would be killed?"

My heart sank. I sat and stared at my mic. I knew that voice. I knew it was Kyle. Simply hearing his voice made me ache.

"Yes." I cleared my throat. "Yes, I was notified by the creator of Venergy at the beginning of my investigation that he was threatened not to speak to anyone about the cancer risk. He was afraid of me because I was associated with the company. Then, people started disappearing and dying. I did not want anyone else to know, no one, because I wanted to protect them. I felt I had already killed my brother, and I did not want to be responsible for the death of another one of my loved ones."

The caller did not respond. The DJ asked if he had any other questions, but the caller quietly replied, "No," and hung up.

I felt a sort of nervous satisfaction at having been able to tell Kyle the reasons for my secrecy and my actions. I wondered if he cared to ask because he still loved me, or if he was only curious. I wondered if he realized I had done the best I could do.

We finished the required reporting time and I left the studio. Now I was permitted to be interviewed by national media, so the next week was going to be filled with interviews across the country, from California to New York.

After grabbing an iced tea and some treats for my parents, I returned home. We spent the entire day cleaning and dividing out Joey's things. It was an exhausting, numbing task. That night, we were so tired that we all went straight to bed without as much telling each other goodnight.

The next morning, we spent a few hours at my brother's house before we returned home so my parents could dress for Kyle's wedding.

My mom came into the kitchen wearing a beautiful dark green dress. "I bought this when I thought I would be the mother of the bride," she said with her nose scrunched.

"It's beautiful, Mom." I tried to keep her from feeling bad. My parents kept insisting they could skip the wedding, but I knew they wanted to go, so the best I could do was act like I didn't care at all.

My dad wore his best jeans, and he tucked in his best button-up plaid shirt. He kissed my forehead and said that Kyle was making the biggest mistake of his life, that Kyle did not deserve me. I hugged him, and then they left.

I considered working at Joey's house and surprising my parents with all the work I had done on my own, but the thought of being in that empty place all alone made me feel sick. The day was too hard for me to be productive. So, I did what I always did when I needed time to myself or to clear my head. I ran.

I grabbed my earbuds, pulled my hair into a ponytail, tied on running shoes and I ran out of my parents' house. I ran and ran. After an hour of pushing on without any destination, I noticed I was running past the Baptist church where Kyle was getting married. The parking lot was full. I looked at my watch—still thirty minutes until the service began.

I ran past the church, then turned around and ran back. I opened one of the front doors, then backed away from them. *What am I doing?* I thought.

I jogged out of the parking lot and away from the church. Then, as if Joey was taunting me from heaven, my Pandora station blaring in my earphones played "You Don't Know Me." I vividly remembered me and Kyle dancing at the restaurant on the pier, how he held me close and promised me that he would always love me. I remembered listening to that song for years, thinking of the impossible possibility of us being together.

Defeated, I walked back through the church parking lot and threw open the front door. I pulled my earbuds, out but the song continued to play—I could hear the tune playing softly from the speakers resting on my shoulders. I stood in front of the doors to the auditorium. The last time I had walked through these doors had been the last time I saw my brother.

I gently opened one door only enough to fit my body through. I stood against it and breathed in the scene. I could hear nothing but the pulse of the music on my shoulders as Kyle faced Janet, holding her hands while the preacher behind them faced the congregation.

I looked at my parents, at the empty space next to them. I looked back at Kyle, and all I heard resonating from my earphones was the song, our song.

Kyle looked at me, then he said shifted on his feet and said something to Janet. Then he looked at me again. Then Janet looked at me. The entire audience turned and looked at me, and the song ended.

Silence.

I ran. I ran through the hall and out of the church, desperate to get away from all of those eyes watching me. I cried as I ran. I wiped the tears, snot, and sweat with the bottom of my shirt.

After what must have been an hour of aimless running, I retreated back to my parents' house. My parents' car was home, so I figured they had not spent a lot of time at the reception. I opened the door to the house, and sitting at the kitchen table was Kyle. He was in his suit and tie that we had picked out for our wedding. He stood the second he saw me. I did not see a wedding ring on his finger.

I didn't move. We stared at each other without a word. Kyle wiped his hands on his pant legs, and then he walked over to me and dropped to one knee.

"Kat, I made a huge mistake," he said in a rush. "I should have never tried to marry Janet. I should have supported you when you needed me. I should have understood why you didn't tell me, or have at least tried to understand you. I was upset about losing Joey and scared when I saw you shooting that car. I was scared for you when you left the day Joey died." Kyle began to cry, but he did not get up.

"I went after you when you left, and I heard everything you said about Venergy. I was angry that you had said nothing to me, that you hadn't trusted me enough to confide in me and to let me to be there for you. I didn't know how I could marry a woman who didn't trust me, so I went back to Janet. I asked her to marry me, and she said yes."

He shook his head, still in tears. "I was running away. I was a coward. I was wrong, and I hurt you. I am so sorry. Please, forgive me. Please say you will give me another chance. Let me spend the rest of our lives making it up to you."

I took Kyle's hands and pulled him to his feet. Tears were dripping off his chin and landing on our clasped fingers. I hugged him tight for a long moment. Then I pulled back and grabbed his hands again.

"Kyle, I love you," I said. "I always have and I always will. I forgive you. You lost your best friend, I was acting crazy, and there was so much going on at once. I'm not mad at you."

Kyle squeezed my hands and his lips pursed in a tight half-smile. I held him tight.

"But you didn't support me when I needed you." His smile started to fade. "You didn't care for me when my brother was dead. You didn't bail me out of that jail cell. You left me there. Even if you were mad at me, even if you planned to break up with me, how hard was it to understand how scared I was? After my parents bailed me, you never contacted me to make sure I was safe, to see if I even had a job or a career anymore.

He was watching me with wide eyes, but I kept going. I would not lie to him again. "I will always love you, Kyle, but I have to protect myself. I don't know if I could ever live a life with you. I feel like you abandoned me when I needed you most."

I let go of his hands, and then walked to my room and shut the door, pressing my back to it. After a few moments of silence, I heard the front door close and I knew he had left. I curled up my bed and cried for hours. I had no room for Kyle in my life anymore. My life was MedVasive now.

38

Over the next week and a half, I spent twelve hours a day reviewing and researching new products. I was interviewed on the Today Show, Good Morning America, and multiple other broadcasts. One day, I gave seven interviews in eight hours. I promoted Molly, discussed my investigation of Venergy, and gave tribute and condolences to individuals who had been harmed. I attempted to name different victims in every interview to drive home my sincerity. I made it clear every time I spoke that MedVasive would have never harmed anyone. David and Darren were fully and completely responsible, and they were being held accountable.

My interview with Dr. Oz was particularly stressful. He had Oprah on satellite, and I apologized to her and to Dr. Oz's audience for the dangers to which I had exposed them.

Oprah hailed me a pioneer and stated she was proud of me, not only for unveiling the sins of the founders of MedVasive, but for sticking with the company in an attempt to revive it. I was overwhelmingly relieved and surprised that she was not angry with me.

Dr. Oz and I discussed the importance of thorough research and investigation into pharmaceutical and medical devices, and then I spoke of Molly for several minutes.

Dr. Oz had two more minutes of the segment, and I was finally ready to relax, ready for the interview to be over. "So," Dr. Oz said, "last time you were here, I believe we witnessed a proposal. And of course, you said yes." The crowd cheered. "So have you set a wedding date? I bet he is so proud of you."

My smile melted. "Actually..." I glanced at the audience, then back at the host. "Actually, I didn't tell him about my investigation of Venergy. I didn't tell him about any of it. Kyle—uh, that's his name. He, um, found out when everyone else found out, when I was on the radio the day my brother died. He felt like I hadn't been honest with him, so we broke up."

The crowd had mixed reactions to that. I tried to ignore them, feeling my face heat up.

Dr. Oz asked if I had attempted to speak to him since the decision to stay with the company. I sat up straight and said, "We agree that I needed to focus on MedVasive right now."

The crowd was silent, and Dr. Oz did not immediately comment. Finally, Oprah chimed in, and I had to fight back a sigh of relief.

"You were brave, Kathy," she said. "Reviving MedVasive is

going to take plenty of time and energy, all of which you are going to have to dedicate. Love is not a fairytale, especially for women in positions such as us."

I thanked her and nodded my agreement, but I did not smile.

The camera focused close to Dr. Oz's face, he pointed to it and announced, "Next, we will have a professional groomer show us how to groom our pets without flaring up those pesky allergies. You won't want to miss the little critters we're going to have on the show when we come back from this short break."

I was ushered off the stage by the stage hands without any fanfare. I went to the back room for my things and took a second to look at myself in the brightly lit mirror. I wasn't sure I recognized the woman looking back at me.

I missed Kyle. This interview had been hard—it had reminded me of how happy Kyle and I ere, back when he was my biggest supporter. Until now, I mostly had just felt sad about him and guilty for messing up our relationship. Now, I looked at myself and tried to settle things.

I would be alone now, and busy, and that would be okay.

I left the studio and walked down the street to burn time until my next interview. I missed my brother, and wished I could call him to vent about the whole Kyle situation and about my fears for the future of my company. Joey would assure me that I could revive MedVasive and that I would not be lying flat on my face in a year.

Although my brother may have been gone, there was a sense of relief in moving forward, moving into the future. I was closing a chapter of my life. I was closing the Venergy chapter, that of my brother's cancer, that of my love life, and that of a naïve woman who trusted too much and thought too little. I was a new person, a stronger person. I knew I was still growing into her, but Kathy Bishop was changing from a doubtful and worrisome professional to a fearless woman who would do anything and everything. When death and failure were no longer frightening, unfamiliar consequences, then a person could truly change. I was changing.

I wandered the streets of New York City and took in the smells and watched the people. I looked into every shop I passed. I walked past a tattoo shop, and then I walked back to it. I threw open the door and found myself in a small room with two salon chairs in the midst of the black and white art hanging all over the walls.

The man standing behind a glass table covered in books of sample tattoos asked if he could help me. I asked him to scrawl *can't stop, won't stop* on the inside of my left arm.

This was the beginning of the new Kathy Bishop and she would never stop, not for anything.

39

I never called Kyle again after his non-wedding to Janet. I didn't let myself.

He never called me either.

My parents never asked me about it, and we never spoke of Kyle. I saw him at my parents' church when I visited Dade City on the weekends but we never spoke, and I refused to look at him, even when his silhouette burned in my peripheral. For months, I dreamed of him interrupting church service and begging me to come back to him.

I saw him at the store when my mom and I shopped together. I stayed clear of the pharmacy, but I stole a peek at him every time. One day, my mom mentioned that she and Kyle never discussed me when she picked up Dad's prescriptions.

After several months, it became obvious to everyone that

Kyle and I were over for good. I never heard that he found someone new, and I never saw him with any other girl at church. But it did not matter to me.

God gave me the gift of solidarity. I kayaked, ran, traveled, and during all of it, I mastered the art of being alone. I was an avid reader and I could get lost in a book—the relationships in my books would satisfy any small need for one of my own that crept up now and again.

In the end, the FDA approved Molly, and virtually all pediatricians recommended it to parents of children between six months and a year. We had yet to receive any reports of problems other than a few red rashes at shot sites. Molly helped pull the company stock out of the ground. The stock and the value of MedVasive was still less than half of what it was prior to the Venergy debacle, but it was on the rise.

It took me months to hire a new assistant. I finally found a young girl who was eager to learn and seemed ambitious enough to work at the speed and hours that were necessary. It would not be the same as having Sandy, but I knew the new girl would grow to be an impressive assistant.

I spent a lot of my time handling the legal claims filed on a daily basis related to Venergy and several of our other old products. Our legal funds, which were set aside, were utterly depleted. The insurance company that provided coverage for MedVasive filed suit against us, claiming it should not have to pay for any of the suits because of Darren and David's intentional fraud. They dropped our coverage, and I knew the road to finding a new insurance company to cover us would be a long one, but we would make it. We would.

Darren and David were convicted of multiple felony crimes, and they were sentenced to hard labor in prison for three fifty-year terms. They would never see freedom another day in their lives. I was sad for them in some way, but justice had been served for my brother, for Sandy, for of the victims in Louisiana, and for all of the people who were bringing claims against the company.

In the midst of the flurry that was my life, I made sure to visit my parents once or twice a month. Slowly, but surely, both of them were getting their spirits back. They sold Joey's home and put pictures of him all over their house, just as I had done to mine.

The first Thanksgiving without Joey was hard. Christmas was almost unbearable. Easter was easier on us, but not by much. There was always an empty seat at the table that could not be overlooked.

Kyle stopped visiting my parents, no matter whether I was there or not. Apparently, he had left my parents to themselves after our last conversation. They never spoke of that conversation, or of the boy who had been like a son to them.

On Joey's birthday, we visited his grave with bundles of balloons, cupcakes, and a small radio. We played his favorite music while we ate, and then we let the balloons fly to the sky.

My work calendar was full of promotions of the new products we were putting on the market, but I kept three days free for the next month: the day prior to that of my brother's death, the anniversary, and the day after.

Despite its ups and downs, I was grateful for God's hand in my life in the past year. I knew I had made the correct decision to stay with MedVasive. A few weeks prior, I had been approached by a publishing company, and now I was working on a book about the Venergy situation and the comeback of MedVasive. They have a writer of their own assisting me in drafting the manuscript. The book would portray me as a brave, powerful woman, an idea that would have embarrassed me a year ago. The old me would have never seen herself as that sort of person. But now, I was that sort of person.

40

It was one year since Joey had died.

My parents had planned a gathering at their house to commemorate. I went to Dade City the day before the memorial to assist my mom in baking and cleaning. I installed speakers around the house that would play Joey's favorite music in the background, and I hung his guitar in the middle of the living room wall.

Before leaving Sarasota, I had made a collage of pictures of my brother at all ages, and even included a picture of Joey when he was near death. He was visibly sick in the photo, but he sat draped in between Kyle and me. He was trying to smile, but it was obviously forced. I placed my creation on the kitchen table.

I spent the remainder of the day talking to my mom and

waiting for my dad to return from horseback riding. When he arrived, we had a nice, quiet dinner. Joey was the one who always asked about my career, and now that he was gone, no one asked.

I went to bed early and fell asleep reading a book. The morning came quick, and my mom was up and moving around the house, a hurricane of preparation.

"How many people are you expecting?" I asked as I wandered out of my room. My mom shrugged her shoulders and guessed around a hundred. "People from the church are bringing casseroles and desserts, so we should have enough food," she reassured me.

I left the house for a Starbucks. I felt a pang of loss for my brother, who used to ride with me on my Starbucks runs. When I returned, I took a shower and dressed in a comfortable pair of fitted skinny jeans and a light blue, short-sleeved sweater top. I slipped on brown strappy heels on my way out to find my parents.

My mom and dad were in the kitchen with two of our neighbors. There was a new casserole dish on the table. I smiled and hugged the older couple, natives of Dade City I had known since I was born. We talked about their chickens and the eggs they were laying as more people started to arrive. Within an hour, there was hardly any room left in the house to stand. There were desserts, casseroles, pies, bottles of soda, and multiple appetizers littered all over. We could have fed the entire neighborhood for a week with all of it, but the entire neighborhood was there anyway.

I was numb throughout the entire thing, a permanent

smile plastered on my face. I was not sad enough to cry, but the event brought me no joy, no peace. I knew these gatherings were good for my mom and that it was important to her, but I hated them. I hated faking it. It upset me when people talked to me about my brother, and it upset me when people talked about themselves. What I wanted most was for no one to talk at all—I wanted quiet and a chance to be alone.

"He is still single," I heard some of the guests whispering about Kyle. "He seems so sad at the pharmacy. He promotes all of MedVasive's products."

"He doesn't like it when we talk to him about you," one lady mentioned to me, and her friend nodded in agreement.

The entire gathering became excruciating fast. After hardly an hour, I made a break for it. I closed myself off in my room and crawled into bed. I grabbed the book I had been reading during my stay, and I spent half an hour regaining the strength to return to the circus outside. When I did poke my head out and make my way back into the crowd, it seemed, impossibly, that there were more people were crammed into my parents' home.

I managed to find my dad sitting on the couch as I passed through the living room, and I patted his head when I went by. In the kitchen, I noticed my mom serving out plates and samples to hungry guests. I offered to help, but she declined. Feeling aimless, I walked through the crowd until I found myself wandering to my brother's room. The door was closed. I presumed my parents had closed it beforehand so no one would go in there. I opened the door and stepped inside, but then I stopped short.

Sitting on my brother's bed was Kyle. No one else was in the room. I hesitated. I didn't know if I should stay or bolt. "Sorry. I, uh…" I started to back out of the room.

"Kat, don't go," he blurted. "Stay. For a moment. Please."

I took a deep breath. I forced my hands to close the door behind me, and I carefully sat myself next to Kyle on the bed. My heart was in my stomach. I felt nauseous. I had no idea what to say, and I was more nervous here in this dark, quiet room than I had been in a very long time.

"So," he started in a low voice, "how have you been?"

"Good, thanks." I rubbed my hands up and down my legs. "You?"

"Kat, don't tell me you've been 'good.' You've had to grieve. You've had to single-handedly having to save your company. Not to mention you've been unhappy with me." He put his hand over my restless ones. I stopped moving.

I looked at him and he looked at me. "God is helping me," I assured him. "Time is helping heal a lot of wounds, and I am very blessed."

Kyle nodded and agreed that time did help heal most wounds. "*Most?*" I asked.

"Yeah, *most.*" He did not elaborate, and I did not ask for it.

We sat in silence for a few minutes. At one point, my mom opened the door with a few friends in tow behind her. Her entrance startled me, and I jumped off the bed. I immediately realized how guilty it made me look. My mom and her friends stopped, looked at the two of us, and excused themselves.

Kyle snorted. "Your mom's probably suspicious now."

"I know," I said with a nervous smile. The two of us started to laugh.

"You remember that time Joey and I put that snake in your bed?" he asked.

I rolled my eyes. "Yeah, that was not funny."

"It was *very* funny."

The more I thought about it, the funnier it did seem, and I settled back onto the bed as laughter overtook me. After a moment, I realized I was the only one laughing. I looked at Kyle, who was watching me with a strangely heavy expression on his face, and my mirth died off.

"What?" I asked.

"I love you, Kat," he said, and my heart clenched. "Whether you love me back doesn't change how I feel. I will live the rest of my life regretting how I treated you, and I will never stop loving you." His eyes grew wet, but he closed them for a second and held the tears at bay.

"I love you too," I whispered. "Last year was too much. There was so much drama and we all made crazy decisions. I...I understand why you did what you did."

"It's no excuse," Kyle interrupted. "If you give me another chance, I will never turn my back on you. I will never let you down again, not if I can help it."

I bit my lip. "I'm a different person than I was last year. I'm stronger, and braver, but I've built walls, Kyle. I've grown colder, I think. I know that no matter how hard I tried to suppress it, my love for you never wavered. I do love you, and I feel it inside me every day, even though I ignore it. I'm afraid that if I that if I let myself love you, that wall will come down and I'll revert to the Kathy I was before. I don't want to be that anymore. I want to be strong."

Kyle held my hands tight. He told me that his love *would* strengthen me, not weaken me. He told me that we would be a team, and there would be nothing missing in our lives if we had each other.

"I love you," I said, my voice thick with emotion. "I love you more than you will ever know."

Kyle kissed me there on Joey's empty bed. We did not talk about marriage or where we would live or whether we would even get married. We were just Kyle and Kat again. We were who we were.

When we left the room to join the crowd, Kyle slipped his hand into mine, and we spent the afternoon talking to the entire town, never letting go of each other.

THE END

Sara Blackwell is an employment lawyer and pioneer for the American worker. She owns her own law firm, runs a not-for-profit organization, Protect US Workers and teaches employment law at University of South Florida. She frequently appears on local and national news outlets to include Fox News and was recently featured on 60 minutes, Michelle Malkin Investigates and PBS To The Contrary. Her mission: fight for America through legal and advocacy avenues. Sara is active, imaginative and motivated to give all she has to give to this life and her three lovely children.

This is Sara's second published book. Contact Sara at Sara@theblackwellfirm.com. Check out her websites www.protectusworkers.org and www.theblackwellfirm.com. Also, you can find her on Facebook, Twitter and LinkedIn.